"Think, Lark. Think what's at stake!"

Lark wanted to think, but she couldn't. How much was too much? In her desire to be a dutiful daughter, was she going too far? She must have time and space to figure that out. Until she did, she couldn't take the final walk down the aisle to bind her life inextricably to the man her father had chosen.

And she remembered standing there, alone in a crowd, wondering where she should go and what she should do next. While she debated with herself, an image rose up before her.

Jared Wolf. She realized that the boy she'd always remembered had grown into a *man*, a man she knew instinctively she'd never forget.

Dear Reader,

Harlequin Romance would like to welcome you back to the ranch again with our yearlong miniseries, **HITCHED!** We've rounded up twelve of our most popular authors and the result is a whole year of romance Western style: cool cowboys, rugged ranchers and, of course, the women who tame them.

So look out for books branded **HITCHED!** in the coming months. We'll be featuring books by Val Daniels, Heather Allison and Barbara McMahon to name but a few!

Happy reading, partners!

The Editors,
Harlequin Romance

How the West was wooed!

Runaway Wedding
Ruth Jean Dale

Harlequin Books

TORONTO • NEW YORK • LONDON
AMSTERDAM • PARIS • SYDNEY • HAMBURG
STOCKHOLM • ATHENS • TOKYO • MILAN
MADRID • WARSAW • BUDAPEST • AUCKLAND

ISBN 0-373-03413-X

RUNAWAY WEDDING

First North American Publication 1996.

CHAPTER ONE

SOMEONE had been sitting in Jared Wolf's chair.

The wooden rocker, like most of the furniture in Wolf Cabin, had been hand-hewn by his ancestors and he knew every inch of it, every curve and angle and nick and splinter. He knew exactly where each piece belonged in the room, for he had been the one who restored each item to its rightful place.

The minute he lit the kerosene lamp, he knew that one particular rocking chair had been moved nearer the window, as if to catch the final rays of a sun set hours ago. All his senses sprang to instant alertness.

Carrying the lamp, he entered the kitchen, moving with silent caution. Concentration total, he looked around the room...and the hair on the nape of his neck prickled.

Someone had been eating his food. An open can of pork 'n' beans stood on the wooden countertop. In the tin dishpan rested a small bowl and one fork.

Adrenaline pumped through his body. In a single noiseless bound, he crossed the room and slipped up the stairs to his bedroom. Holding the lamp high, he eased the door open.

Someone had been sleeping in his bed, he saw at once.

And she still was...

"Wake up, Goldilocks."

The harsh voice penetrated Lark Mallory's sleeping consciousness well before its meaning sank in. Uncertain for a moment where she was, she struggled to open her eyes so she could assess this new threat. Had her father found her already? Not that! After all she'd gone through to reach refuge, that couldn't be happening to her.

"Come on, open your eyes," the voice resumed with even more impatience. "Papa Bear's home and none too happy to find a stranger in his bed."

A hand gripped her shoulder and flipped her over onto her back. Her eyes flew open involuntarily, in fright and shock, and she looked up at the most intimidating man she'd ever seen.

His dark presence filled the small bedroom. Illuminated only by the faint glow of a lamp held aloft in one hand, his face was a mysterious blend of light and shadow that emphasized impossibly high cheekbones and a strong cleft chin. Ink-dark hair, shaggy and thick, curled around his ears and over his broad forehead. His nose was strong and well-shaped, his mouth curving and sensuous.

All in all, her startled senses reported, a dangerous and dangerously appealing man. Her heart flip-flopped and she let out a gasp of alarmed acknowledgment of his identity—and of his control of the situation.

His dark eyes glittered. "What in the *hell* are you doing in my bed?"

His raspy tone sent shivers down her back. "I—why, I—I thought—that is, it seemed to me—"

His impatient exclamation brought to a halt her stuttering attempt at an explanation. Distracted and suddenly aware that she'd fallen exhausted into bed wearing only bra and panties, Lark hauled the sheet up over her shoulders and stared helplessly at him.

Swallowing hard, she tried again. "It's me, Lark Mallory," she said in a voice that quavered. "Don't you know me, Jared?"

"I know you," Jared Wolf said.

"Thank heaven!" Relieved, Lark slumped deeper into the bed. "I recognized you right away. How long's it been, Jared?" *As if she'd ever forget.* "Let's see, I was fourteen the last time my family came here, so you must have been...nineteen? And Risa was about the same—"

He set the lamp on the bedside table and reached for the top button of his chambray work shirt. His faint smile was not welcoming.

"—or maybe a year or so younger than you— What do you think you're *doing*?"

He tugged the now-open shirt from the waistband of his trousers, revealing an abdomen ridged with muscle. "Taking off my clothes. That's an innovation of mine—I always do it before climbing into bed."

"But you can't—I mean, where—?" Her horrified glance skittered around the room, as if she might find another bed, another door—another person. "Jared, what's the matter with you? What are you thinking?"

"That I'm tired and I want to go to bed." He dropped the shirt onto the floor.

His torso was as hard and sexy as the rest of him. Lark gaped foolishly—until he reached for the belt buckle at his waist.

"Stop!" Sitting up, she scooted toward the far side of the bed. "I'm really confused, here. This is my bed. I know Father's always let you use the cabin when we weren't here, but—"

"*Let* me use the cabin?"

Jared's jaw tightened and his hands clenched into fists—big fists. He stared at her with condemnation so fierce it made her skin prickle.

Again, he'd managed to confuse her completely. She stumbled over her words. "Well, yes. I mean, we were only here for a few weeks each year, that's true. And then after Mother—but that's not the point. This is the Mallory Cabin so I'm afraid I'll have to ask you to...to please go, because I'll be spending some time here myself this summer."

If she'd thought to dismiss him, her aim came to naught. He rocked back on his heels and his hard mouth twisted.

"The *Mallory* Cabin?"

"W-why, yes, of course."

"This is Wolf Cabin. It's never been the Mallory Cabin, not even when Mallorys were desecrating it. As for your current uninvited presence...aren't you overlooking one little thing?"

She lifted her chin, and the sheet, trying to hide her consternation with bravado. "Such as?"

"Such as asking the owner's permission."

"I hardly think I need my father's permission to—"

"I wasn't referring to Drake Mallory. I said the *owner*."

"But—" She frowned, first puzzled and then... horrified. "No! You don't mean...?"

He smiled with his mouth but not his eyes. "Ah, but I do mean. I'm the owner and have been for years. That's my bed you're in, Goldilocks. Unless you want to share it with me, I suggest you haul your little fanny out of there."

"Oh, good Lord! I can't believe this." Twisting the sheet around her, Lark struggled to her feet. How had a life as well-ordered as hers turned into such a nightmare? "Father never said a word about selling the cabin," she protested. "I mean, we quit coming here for family vacations but I thought he still used it occasionally."

Jared's nod was curt. "He did, for a while. Brought various . . . guests with him, as a matter of fact. He put the place on the market about the time he decided to remarry."

Which made a certain horrible kind of sense to Lark. Her father's second marriage had only lasted for a couple of years. Marsha had definitely not been the kind of woman who'd trek off into the wilderness after any man.

"But—" Lark frowned at Jared Wolf, prepared to argue her case further but suddenly finding herself breathless. Which was ridiculous; she wasn't fourteen anymore, she was twenty-six, a grown woman. She swallowed hard. "Then you bought it back?" she guessed in a weak voice. "You own this cabin now?"

The look of satisfaction on his face spoke volumes. "My mother made a mistake when she let that greedy bastard cheat her out of Wolf Cabin. It took me a while, but now it's mine." His expression made it clear he'd never relinquish ownership of Wolf Cabin again.

Looking at him exude confidence and power, Lark felt an overwhelming sense of hopelessness. Now where would she go? What would she do? How would she find the solitude she so desperately needed to sort out her thoughts and make the most important decision she would ever face?

Jared let out his breath on a note of disgust. "Oh, hell."

She looked up in panic; now what?

He glared at her. "You're trespassing. You know that, don't you?"

"Y-yes, I guess so, if what you've told me is the tru—" The look on his face made her bite off the last word. "All right, yes. I believe you. But I have no place else to go, Jared! I came here because I was desperate to be alone to figure out...well, make some important decisions."

"Tough."

The word was coldly said but she wondered...for just a moment she thought she'd detected a flash of understanding, perhaps even sympathy.

"One night," she bargained. "Let me sleep here tonight and then tomorrow...tomorrow we can talk." In the daylight. *When I don't feel as if I'm locked up in a cage with a mountain lion.*

For a heartbeat, she thought he would yet turn her away, but then the stiff set of those incredibly broad shoulders relaxed. He gave a short nod.

"One night. Then you're out of here."

Relief washed over her. "Thank you," she said sincerely, sitting down abruptly on the edge of the bed. "I knew you couldn't have turned into the kind of man who'd throw a woman out into the night on a mountaintop—"

He was reaching for his belt buckle again.

"*What are you doing?*"

He slipped his belt through its loops and dropped it. "I'm getting ready for bed."

"But didn't you just say—?"

"I said you could stay, but I didn't say I'd go. You happen to be sitting on my bed. Not that I have any objections to sharing...." His dark glance roamed down over her shoulders, bare except for bra straps above the sheet still clutched around her. "If you *do* have objections, I'd suggest you find yourself another place to bunk because in a couple of minutes, I'm going to be buck naked and flat on my back in that bed."

With a squeak of alarm, Lark jumped up and edged toward the door. "But where will *I* sleep?" she protested. "I wouldn't have even come into this room but the other bedroom's full of paint cans and broken furniture."

"Not my problem." He released the snap at his waist.

"At least let me take the lamp so I don't go bumping into things," she pleaded, her gaze on his hands playing with the second snap, hands surprisingly long-fingered and sensitive-looking. When he ceased fiddling with his fly, she felt deep relief.

"Don't set the place on fire," he suggested dryly, offering her the glowing cranberry-glass lamp.

She took it, her hands surrounding its curved base and brushing against his fingers—and she almost dropped the lamp right there. "I—I won't," she promised, her heart pounding with the tension which shot through her. Turning quickly, she hurried toward the door.

"Sleep tight." His voice, lazy and teasing, pursued her down the steep stairs.

"Sleeping tight" seemed out of the question. There wasn't a piece of furniture in the entire cabin—outside his bedroom, of course—fit for sleeping at all. She tried everything before giving up: the small two-seater that couldn't actually be called either a couch or a love seat, since it was far too primitive in its construction; the wooden rocking chair she'd moved earlier for a better view of the glories of a Rocky Mountain sunset; a bench along one wall. She did finally find a blanket to go with her sheet, and in desperation, settled on the sheepskin rug in front of the cold, dark fireplace in the front room.

Blowing out the lamp's small, brave flame at last, she settled into the darkness with an exhausted groan. What a couple of days she'd had! Her problems had been legion without this new wrinkle....

This new wrinkle: Jared Wolf, the boy who'd been the unknowing target of her first girlish crush; the boy she'd always adored. She'd thought him quite the most wonderful boy in the world, and cast him in the leading role of many a youthful fantasy.

Back then, fantasies, like life, were simpler. Time and again, she'd imagined the boy of her dreams appearing at her home in Palm Beach just in time to escort her to the prom, where they'd knock everybody's socks off with their style and elegance; or of him discovering her soaking in the hot springs near the cabin—discreetly clad in a swimsuit, of course; she'd been too young and innocent at the time for anything more risqué. Stripping down to his own swimsuit, he'd wade out to give her a watery kiss....

But only in her dreams. In truth, he'd never paid her the slightest attention, beyond what his job had required.

Lark smiled in the darkness, remembering the time she'd spent here; but slowly the smile slipped away.

This dark and commanding stranger was not much like the quiet and accommodating boy who'd done odd jobs for the Mallorys, including maintenance on the cabin. What had changed him?

Something gouged her hip and she rolled over on her furry pallet, seeking a more comfortable position and failing to find one. A suitable metaphor for her life, she thought gloomily. She desperately needed a few days to get hold of herself and her emotions. Her sister was doubtless right; this malaise was probably nothing more than a case of pre-wedding jitters. If she could just stay out of her father's way until she worked it all out in her head, everything would be all right.

Or would it? What if she decided she couldn't face a lifetime with Wes Sherborn? Would her father ever accept or understand such a decision?

He'd point out the obvious: she and Wes had grown up together, gone to school together, their fathers were in business together, they had been raised with similar values. Worse, they'd practically been betrothed by their families at birth. Wes was tall, blond, handsome. His future in the company was naturally bright.

He also bored her to tears; her problem, not his. She was restless, dissatisfied, feeling trapped and rudderless most of the time. She couldn't blame Wes for that. If she couldn't even name what she wanted, how could he give it to her?

There in the black of night, she flashed on an image of the man in the bed upstairs and a little shiver shot down her spine. No more fantasies about Jared Wolf, she warned herself; that would be far too dangerous now that she was all grown up.

She rolled over onto her stomach and closed her eyes, willing sleep to come. Instead, the events of the past two days unrolled behind her closed eyelids like a filmstrip....

A slender woman in a formal wedding gown stood alone on a plushly carpeted dais in the exclusive bridal shop on Worth Avenue in Palm Beach, Florida. As she pirouetted slowly, the mirrored walls reflected a multitude of beautiful brides, each wearing the same detached expression as the original. Off to one side, two women observed with critical eyes.

"Turn to your right, Lark," the bride-to-be's sister instructed. "I'm not sure the train is draping properly." She glanced at her companion. "What do you think?"

The bridal consultant frowned. "That you're right. Our bride is still losing weight. If this keeps on, we'll never get a proper fit, Mrs. Clarke."

Risa Mallory Clarke shot an *I-told-you-so* glance at the bride in question. "The fit," she said loftily, "will be perfect. The wedding is August thirtieth, which is a mere six weeks away." She patted Lark's cold hand. "You'll stop this nonsense, won't you, dear. Now about that train—"

The two women stepped forward to join the bride on the pale pink carpeting, tugging and pushing, smoothing and patting. Lark stood unmoving, looking through the elegant shop and right on into the future.

Life should be perfect for a privileged young woman engaged to a handsome young man fully prepared and able to provide her with the life-style to which she was accustomed. She should be the happiest woman in the world....

The sensuous glide of the heavy fabric beneath the knuckles of her clenched fists sent a shiver of doubt through her. The gown was beautiful, beyond doubt, but it gave her no pleasure.

"Duchesse satin," Karen Dodd, the wedding consultant, had identified the gleaming cloth, in a shade called "ivory blush." From the corner of one eye, Lark saw mirrored reflections of pleated sleeves, a bodice with lace overlay re-embroidered with pearls, the graceful swirl of an elaborate cathedral train, and two women examining it all as minutely as if it were of cosmic importance.

Finally satisfied, Ms. Dodd went to get the veil while Risa tried to raise her younger sister's spirits. "You're going to be a beautiful bride," she said with a liberal dose of her usual confidence. "Don't pay any attention to *her*. You know what they say."

"No, Risa," Lark murmured without much interest. "What do they say?"

"That a woman can never be too thin or too rich." Risa laughed ruefully. "Actually, I envy you. While you're becoming more and more svelte, I'm getting absolutely tubby."

Lark looked at Risa, elegant in pencil-slim white linen. "I don't think so."

"Well, I am." Risa brushed her fingers across Lark's cheek. "It's not the weight you're losing that concerns me, it's the dark circles under your eyes. Are you all right, Lark? Really all right? We haven't talked about this since Christmas when you got engaged—"

"And there's no need to talk about it now," Lark said quickly.

"Are you sure, Lark? Because if you're not—"

A timely interruption was just what Lark needed, and got when the wedding consultant practically skipped onto the dais. She brought with her a froth of satin-edged lace illusion net. "The crowning touch," she announced, "literally!"

With reverent hands, she lifted the airy confection and placed it on Lark's curly, red-gold hair. With infinite care, she positioned the elegant headpiece of white silk roses, fluffed and arranged the multitiered veil.

"Absolutely gorgeous!" she declared.

Risa nodded agreement. "Lark's going to have a perfect wedding," she predicted, "and a perfect life."

Lark turned slowly to meet the wide hazel eyes of the woman in the mirror. That woman didn't look gorgeous, she looked thin and haggard and... frightened.

That woman didn't look as if she even knew what the word *perfect* meant.

How had she got herself into this mess? Perhaps because an August wedding had seemed a lifetime away when they'd set the date last December. Wes Sherborn had popped the question during the traditional holiday gathering of his family and hers. He'd done it publicly, too, and from the gleeful expressions turned her way, Lark guessed that everyone in the room must have known what was coming... except her.

That realization brought with it a spark of resentment, but then everyone crowded around with hugs and kisses and congratulations, sweeping her along.

Had she actually said "yes"? She couldn't recall saying the word but they all seemed to take it for granted. Looking into her father's beaming face, she'd shoved aside all those niggling little doubts. She'd spent her entire lifetime trying to win that kind of approval from him and she wanted to enjoy it while she could. If she were making a mistake, there'd be time to rectify it before it was too late.

But time had raced past, and with the wedding just around the corner, Lark felt as helpless as the heroine in a melodrama; tied to the railroad tracks, she could only watch her future rush toward her like a runaway locomotive.

The telephone on a desk beside the dais had interrupted her frantic thoughts but only temporarily; it was her father.

"Lark. Glad I caught you." As always, Drake Mallory sounded as if there were at least a dozen things he'd rather be doing. "Be at the house tonight at six. Bring Wes, of course."

The vise around Lark's chest tightened. "But we have plans. We're supposed to—"

"This is important," her father interrupted with brusque impatience. "Wes knows. Be there." He hung up on her.

For a moment she continued to grip the handset so hard her fingers cramped. Then she replaced it in its cradle very carefully. "He wants Wes and me at the house tonight at six," she reported tonelessly. "He sounded even more dictatorial than usual."

"Try to be patient. You know he's got business problems. That accounting thing—"

"I thought that had been taken care of."

"Not really. And unless Father and Mr. Sherborn get to the bottom of it before it becomes public knowledge—" Risa shivered. "Reputation is so important in real estate. With the construction of the new headquarters complex under way, Tony says it would look really bad if this leaked to the press—disastrous is what he actually said."

"Well, I'm not likely to tell anyone. Besides, if it isn't that it's something else. I just tense up when he starts snapping out orders."

"You could try to be a little more understanding."

"I will, just as soon as you tell me what's going on. Why have Wes and I been summoned to appear tonight?"

The usually outspoken Risa had prevaricated. "I'm sure it's nothing to worry about. Come over here and let me check that train again. It still isn't right."

"The train is fine. What's going on, Risa?"

"Lark, you're putting me in a tight spot. Father will be furious if I say another word. Why not wait and be surprised?"

Lark wouldn't, and eventually, she wore Risa down.

"But you made me do it," Risa sighed. "Father and Wes's dad are giving you two your wedding presents tonight. Father's gift is the key to a house—and it's a great house, Lark, you'll love it. Right on the beach, gated, the whole thing. Mr. Sherborn's giving *each* of you your own key—to his-'n'-hers BMWs—plus a fabulous honeymoon on a private yacht in the Greek Isles. Is this fabulous or what?"

With every word her sister uttered, Lark felt her shackles tightening. Heavy satin twisted beneath her clenching hands. This represented the final indignity: cloned automobiles, a honeymoon of someone else's choosing, and a house she'd never seen but which she was expected to share with Wes as man and wife.

Man and wife. She hadn't even learned to be her own woman. How could she be Wes Sherborn's wife?

Lark had climbed into her car with Risa's pleas ringing in her ears. "Promise you'll be there! If you're not, Father will kill me! This is nothing but a bad case of bridal nerves, Lark. Believe me, all women go through it."

"You didn't."

"Remind me to tell you about that someday."

"I will. Now I've got to go."

"Not until you promise! Think, Lark. Think what's at stake!"

Lark wanted to think, but she couldn't. How much was too much? In her desire to be the dutiful daughter her father wanted, was she going too far? She must have time and space to figure that out. Until she did, she couldn't take the final walk down the aisle to bind her life inextricably with that of the man her father had chosen.

So when she drove away from the bridal shop, she didn't head toward home but turned into traffic on a broad, palm-lined boulevard. She'd grown up in southern Florida, spent practically her entire life here. She'd lived in her father's house on Jupiter Island for years, except for the brief stint after her parents' divorce when she went with her mother to a Miami condo. She was intimately accustomed to Florida's heat, to the humidity, the palm trees, the sand.

She was *not* accustomed to the incredible pressure that had been building since she and Wes became engaged. As the breakneck pace of preparations for the big day gathered momentum, she'd felt her life careening out of control, until now she found herself driving much too fast down a freeway heading for she knew not where.

A sign indicated the exit to Palm Beach International Airport and Lark whipped the steering wheel to the right. She might not know where she was going but she'd get there faster on an airplane.

Lark had called home from Dallas-Fort Worth International Airport. Waiting anxiously for someone to answer, she watched travelers steam past on the concourse. A clock suspended from the ceiling in the middle of the corridor told her the time: nine-fifteen, ten hours since she'd left the bridal shop.

A maid answered on the fifth ring.

Lark spoke in a voice several notches lower than her normal tone. "This is Ms. Dodd, Miss Mallory's wedding consultant, calling for Mrs. Clarke."

"One moment please."

Lark waited, wondering how she'd ever explain what she was doing in Dallas. She didn't know *herself* what she was doing in Dallas. She'd walked up to the first airline counter she'd seen at Palm Beach International and bought a ticket on the first available plane.

That plane happened to be going to Dallas.

Now what? She didn't know a soul in Dallas, had never spent any time here except in this same airport. For the few years her family had owned the vacation cabin in the Rocky Mountains of Colorado, their route had invariably led through Dallas, then on to Colorado Springs where her father rented a van for the drive into the mountains.

She felt a nostalgic pleasure at the memories. Her mother had been alive then, her parents' marriage intact. She had wandered the piney woods, bathed in the hidden hot springs, fallen in love for the first time. A smile tugged at her lips. He'd been the handsomest boy. She'd cried when her father said they wouldn't be going back to the mountains. For years afterward, she'd thought of Jared Wolf, wondering—

"Ms. Dodd? This really isn't a good time—"

"Risa! It's me, Lark."

A gasp was quickly followed by, "Oh, my God! Where are you? Father's going berserk—no, don't tell me! He'd have the police drag you home before you knew what hit you. Just tell me this—are you all right?"

"I'm fine. Or maybe fine's an overstatement. Risa, I don't think I can go through with it."

"Go through with what?"

"The wedding. I don't think Wes is the man for me."

After a long silence, Risa whispered, "You said 'think.' That means you're not sure."

"Well, I'm pretty sure."

"Pretty sure isn't sure enough." Risa groaned. "My God, do you know what pandemonium you've created here? Father's in a rage, Mr. Sherborn got mad and went home, Mrs. Sherborn was crying—"

"And Wes— What about Wes?" Lark interrupted, filled with guilt because she hadn't inquired about him first.

"He waited a couple of hours, then went off to play tennis."

Which was no more than Lark expected. Wes wasn't one to let little things upset him. "I'm sorry I've made everyone unhappy," she said in a thin voice. "I'm ashamed to say, I panicked."

"How do you feel now?"

"Better." Lark bit her lip. "That's a lie. I only feel better because I'm here instead of there. The basic problem is a long way from resolution." She swallowed hard, then blurted, "Risa, what should I do? I'm so confused. I can't think straight anymore."

Risa groaned. "I only know one thing for sure—you don't want to come home until Father's cooled off. Why don't you just stay wherever you are for a day or two? No pressure...just sleep, swim, sun, whatever relaxes you. I'll tell Father you called, but I'll tell him tomorrow or the next day, when he's calm enough to hear me."

"O-OK. I guess that would be best. I... I'm really sorry about this, Risa."

"Don't worry about it. Uhhh...will you call Wes?"

Lark closed her eyes, damning her cowardice. "Would you mind doing it for me? Tell him...just tell him I had to get away from all the pre-wedding pressure for a few days, that I'm fine and will be in touch eventually."

"All right. And, Lark? Take care. We may drive you crazy sometimes but we're still your family and we love you."

"Th-thanks for reminding me." Lark had hated what she had to say next. "One more thing. My car's parked at the airport in Palm Beach. In the glove compartment you'll find the parking ticket and—" She hesitated, then added in a rush, "—my engagement ring. I'd feel safer if you'd pick it up and hang on to it until—"

"Oh, Lark! Don't—"

"I'll be in touch soon."

The filmstrip unrolling in Lark's mind was running down as sleep crept up on her at last. But she remembered how she'd felt when she hung up: terrible.

And she remembered standing there, alone in a crowd, wondering where she should go and what she should do next. While she debated with herself, an image of a log cabin tucked into a shady glen deep in the Rocky Mountains rose before her. The front door opened and a figure stepped out onto the porch.

Jared Wolf. Drifting on the edges of consciousness, she realized that the boy she'd always remembered had grown into a *man*, a man she knew instinctively she'd never forget.

It had taken only one brief encounter for her girlhood crush to blossom into a full-blooded attraction.

CHAPTER TWO

LARK awakened before dawn. By the time the first golden rays crept through the window, she knew what she had to do, at least for the short term: stay. There was nowhere else she could go. No matter what it took, she had to convince Jared to let her remain in Wolf Cabin for a few days.

She was even willing to pay him for that privilege, although he'd have to wait for his money. Unfortunately, she had very little cash left after taking a plane from Florida to Dallas, from Dallas to Colorado Springs, spending a night in a motel there, buying a few necessities, then renting a car for the drive up the mountain.

She had credit cards, of course, but if she used them she felt sure her father would find her in nothing flat. She knew his methods too well; he'd hire detectives, call in favors, do anything he had to do to achieve his own ends. And she knew what those ends would be; get the wandering daughter back home and safely married.

The hell of it was, she knew he'd believe he was doing it for her own good. Well, if she decided to marry Wes, she wanted to do it for *herself*, not her father.

Footsteps on the stair startled her. She rolled over onto an elbow, clutching the sheet around her, wondering if Jared was going to start thinking it was some

24

sort of uniform. He paused at the bottom of the stairs to look in her direction.

What he saw she could only imagine, but whatever it was, it made him smile. "I slept like a log," he announced. "How about you?" His suggestive gaze took in her position on the floor.

Indignation heated her cheeks. "I slept like a rock," she countered, "or on one—I'm not sure which."

He laughed. The sound was so unexpected that she blinked in surprise. Levity softened his features, which only made him that much more compelling. This was the handsome boy she remembered.

She felt herself melting, realized what was happening and stiffened. Why didn't he frown or say something offensive? The way his laughter cut through her defenses was absolutely unnerving.

"Want something to eat before you leave?" he asked. Without waiting for her response, he disappeared into the kitchen.

Once more he'd surprised her, this time unpleasantly. As he passed from sight, she leapt to her feet, sheet intact, and sprinted up the stairs. There she threw on jeans and a new blue T-shirt she'd bought yesterday in Colorado Springs. Within five minutes, she joined Jared in the small kitchen.

He sat at the table with a mixing bowl, a plastic jug of milk and a box of cereal before him, a tablespoon in his hand. Coffee perked on the wood cook stove, and the aroma made her stomach growl.

"Bowls are there." He gestured toward wooden shelves along one wall. "Spoons are in the top drawer. Help yourself."

She did, feeling clumsy and uncertain beneath his level gaze. When at last she sat across from him, she considered the box of cereal with distaste. "At the risk of sounding picky, is that all you have?"

His shuttered expression never changed. "At the risk of sounding indifferent to your problems, it's all I want." He scooped up another spoonful. "Something wrong with it?"

"Oh, no, not at all. It reminds me of twigs and bark, that's all."

"You ever eat twigs and bark?" The chocolate-brown eyes were mesmerizing.

"N-no, but if I ever did, that's what I *think* they'd taste like." Curiosity made her add, "Did you?"

"Did I what?" Deliberately he laid his spoon beside the bowl and reached for the cereal box for a refill.

"Ever eat twigs and bark."

"Sure." Was that genuine humor in his face? "Twigs, bark, and little girls like you—mostly for breakfast, so watch out."

She didn't doubt it for a minute. He offered her the box; pretending a coolness she didn't feel, she accepted and poured a couple of inches in the bottom of her bowl.

He glanced at the stove. "Coffee's ready," he said.

She arched her brows in question; *so*?

"So pour us some," he ordered. "Even you rich kids know how to pour coffee, right?"

"In case you haven't noticed, I'm not a kid anymore," she protested.

"I'm trying *not* to notice." His dark gaze flicked over her so explicitly that she shivered; he noticed, all right. "Cups are over there," he added, returning to his breakfast.

Trembling with awareness, Lark poured the coffee. Why was he treating her this way? She couldn't think of anything she'd ever said or done to offend him. And even if she had, they hadn't met for a dozen years. Who held a grudge for twelve years? she wondered as she poured the coffee.

He didn't offer thanks, just picked up the tin cup and sipped.

"Jared," she began, screwing up her courage, "we have to talk."

All of a sudden the face was as impassive as it had been last night. His complete attention hit her an almost physical blow and for a moment she felt disoriented and at a loss for words.

She saw no reason to mince words so she said, "I'm throwing myself on your mercy, Jared. You've got to let me stay here for a few days."

His expression became even more stony. "*Got* to?"

Lark dug her nails into her palms. "I won't get in your way, I promise. I didn't come all the way to Colorado for company—just the opposite."

Her impassioned words made no visible impact on him. "*Got* to?" he repeated.

She stared down at restless, twisting fingers. "Poor choice of words. It's just that I'm desperate. I don't have anywhere else to go—"

"You really expect me to believe that?"

"—and I'm running out of money—"

"Hold it. You *are* still a Mallory, right? I heard about your daddy's new multimillion-dollar construction project so I know he's still got mega-bucks." His eyes narrowed. "Or is it a husband you're hiding out from? You're not wearing a wedding ring but that's no guarantee nowadays."

She felt a brief flash of pleasure that he'd checked for a wedding band, quickly followed by guilty relief that she'd left her engagement ring in Florida. "I'm not married," she said, which was true; she failed to add that she was engaged, since that seemed beside the point.

"Jeez, you're not in trouble with the law."

"Oh, no, nothing like that. It...it's my father I'm trying to avoid. I've done something..." she cast about for a way to gain Jared's support without revealing too much "...or I'm about to do something, or about *not* to do something— Jared, he'll kill me if he catches up with me before he has a chance to cool off and I have a chance to figure out what I ought to do!"

That last part came out a lot more passionately than she liked, and she hung her head in defeat. He wasn't going to let her stay. She'd just have to use her credit cards to get back to Florida, where she'd be swept off her feet and back onto the same old emotional treadmill.

"Look at me, Lark Mallory."

Surprised at the low, smoky note in his voice, she did as he commanded. For the first time since he'd walked back into her tangled life, she felt a faint flicker of hope. "Yes?" she whispered.

"Does your father know you're here?"

She licked her lips but it never occurred to her to lie to him, for he would surely know. "No. No, he doesn't."

"If he did, would he come after you?"

She closed her eyes and nodded. "I think so. I'm pretty sure—yes. Yes, of course he would." Her eyes flew open again. "But please believe me, I'm not doing this to hurt him, or anyone, for that matter. I'm doing it—I want to do it—to help *myself*. I need space, time, thinking room. And it seemed to me that by coming back to the mountains, a place where I was once truly happy—'' She groaned. ''Oh, how can I possibly make you understand?''

''Don't even try.''

He stood up; she'd lost.

''Don't try because I already understand, far better than you know. Mountains do things to people, whether they realize it or not. No one, good or bad, can see a mountain and not be changed by the experience.'' He took a step toward the doorway. ''You spent enough time here... Yeah, I can understand you running back.''

''Then you won't throw me out?'' she cried after his retreating form.

He flung open the front door, never looking back. ''I didn't say that.''

''I'll pay you, if you'll let me stay. I don't have much cash with me but you know I'm good for it.''

''Now you've gone and insulted me.'' His lip curled contemptuously. ''You Mallorys think everything has its price.'' He walked out.

The door swung closed behind him. She was alone, with no idea what her fate would be.

Jared jumped off the porch and swung sharply to his left, toward the young aspen forest rising from the ridge behind the cabin. The aspens had sprung up in the wake of a fire that had cleared out the lodgepole pines and the ponderosas, a fire that had threatened the cabin itself.

A fire caused by Drake Mallory's carelessness, only one of many reasons Jared carried such a heavy grudge against the man.

A wild garden bloomed beneath the lacy leaves of the trees. Fireweed struck sparks in the sunlight, pearly everlastings waved puffy white heads, and butter-yellow sunflowers shouted for attention.

Jared took in his surroundings with an almost sensual pleasure, although his mind was on what he had just learned.

So little Lark Mallory wanted to avoid her father, did she? Jared could help her to do that...if he chose. The possibilities were positively tantalizing. Although he had no interest in doing favors for the daughter of the man he despised, he might hide her just to irritate that bastard, Mallory.

Jared turned on the ridge to look down on the cabin. Her rental car was parked around back; that's why he hadn't seen it last night.

Why she was running from her father was of little importance to Jared, although he supposed she had good reason. He'd noticed she seemed unsure of herself now, hesitant and unhappy. He remembered her as energetic and cheerful, a happy kid with a ready smile. What had happened to change her?

Not that it mattered, he reminded himself abruptly. If he let her stay, it wouldn't be for her purposes but for his. He leaned a palm against the soft white bark of an aspen and stared out across the valley.

He'd promised his mother that he would not actually pursue his enemy to extract the revenge he craved. Although he loved his mother with all his heart, that was the most Jared had been able to do to ease her mind—and it had, for she had not seen behind his carefully chosen words.

He had *not* promised to forget the many affronts to his family honor. He had never said he forgave the

man, because that would have been—would still be—
a lie.

Jared Wolf had bided his time, waiting for opportunity to present itself. Now his patience had been
rewarded and he found himself firmly in the catbird
seat. If he kept Lark here, he'd be able to draw
Mallory to him whenever he wanted.

He smiled. What a difference a day makes.

He'd stopped by Cripple Creek yesterday afternoon
on his trek into the mountains from Denver. His sister
and her young son were the joy of his life; with them,
he could relax and be himself as he could with no one
else.

Swinging his two-year-old nephew high into the air,
Jared relished the child's delighted shrieks. Little Jared
knew no fear, and if his fiercely protective uncle had
anything to say about it, never would.

"Don't get too rowdy, Uncle Jared," a light voice
instructed from behind them. "It's almost his
bedtime. If you get him too wound up, he'll never get
to sleep."

Jared turned to match Jenny's smile with one of
his own. At twenty-three, his sister was eight years
younger than he, but they'd always been close despite
the age difference. Over the past several years he'd
learned to respect her as well as love her. It wasn't
easy for a woman to raise a child alone, but she was
doing it, and doing a damned fine job, too.

Laughing, she came down off the porch of her small
frame cottage, bare feet sinking into the scraggly grass.
Snatching the plump toddler from Jared's arms, she
planted teasing kisses on his apple cheeks. Her long,
straight hair, black as her brother's, swung around

mother and child in a silken curtain. When she smiled, her eyes, a brilliant blue instead of Little Jared's amber brown, sparkled.

"Can you stay and eat with me?" she asked her brother, clutching the still-giggling child to her chest.

"I'd like to." He hesitated, glancing toward the distant peaks of the Sangre de Cristo mountains, visible to the west of Cripple Creek. The historic Colorado gold-mining town nestled in a volcanic bowl deep in the Rockies, almost 10,000 feet above sea level. Jenny had moved here shortly after Little Jared's birth, judging it a good place to raise a child.

Jared figured the same. Leaning over, he dropped a kiss on his sister's gleaming hair. "Sorry, don't have time to stay for supper."

She pouted prettily. "You headed back to Denver?"

He shook his head and nodded westward.

"The cabin," she said.

"Yes. Got some thinking to do. Need solitude to do it in."

Jenny sat down on the porch step, perching her son on her knees. "Still haven't decided?"

"No." He sat beside her.

"Why not, Jared? It's not like you to be indecisive."

That pricked him, because it was true. "It's a big step, Jen. I built Wolf Cache Systems from the ground up. Yeah, I don't get the same charge out of it I used to, but there's nothing better on the horizon."

"You could get a life, big brother." She spoke softly, but her eyes narrowed purposely. "Take the money and run. You could travel, restock the old homeplace, do some ranching, start another company." She leaned over to kiss his cheek. "You could even find a nice girl and fall in love—or let her find you."

"Jennifer," he said, "you've been reading too many romance novels." He tweaked Little Jared's ear lightly, returned the boy's broad grin, and stood up. "I've got to pick up a few more supplies before I head on to the cabin, so I'd better get a move on. Anything I can do for you before I go?"

"Nope. You've already done it all."

She stood up, leaning over to set the toddler on his feet. Jared reached for the wallet in his hip pocket. "Need any—?"

"No, I don't need a handout," she said rather sharply. "Little Jared and I are doing fine, thank you very much."

He hesitated with the wallet in his hand. "Are you sure? I'd like to help out a little more, if you'd let me."

"Forget it. You've already done too much." She flapped her hands toward his Land Rover parked near the gate to the small fenced yard. "Go on, hibernate up there in that little ol' cabin all summer, see if we care."

But she said it with good humor and he drove away wishing she'd let him do more for her and the boy. He'd bought the little house for them, and he'd already set up a trust fund which would assure the child's education. Other than that, Jenny insisted on making her own way.

As did Jared. Proud self-reliance was a Wolf family trait. Perhaps it came from their Ute Indian great-grandfather, or their feisty Irish great-grandmother, but brother and sister had it—in spades.

He bought supplies in Cripple Creek before heading for the cabin, since the little Mountain Mom 'n' Pop Store would be closed before he reached it. Everything stowed in the back of his vehicle, Jared headed for home. That's what Wolf Cabin was and always would be to him. Even during the years it had been out of the family, it had exerted an almost mystical pull on him. The cabin so lovingly built by his great-grandfather had always been a place of refuge to Jared.

Until that son of a bitch Mallory got his hands on it.

Getting the cabin back after years of humiliation had given Jared more satisfaction than anything he'd ever done. Certainly it had meant more to him than building his own computer tape storage company into a multimillion-dollar organization from the ground up. He enjoyed his business, was proud of what he'd accomplished, but mostly it had been a means to an end.

Making Mallory pay would give Jared almost as much satisfaction as he'd got from reclaiming his birthright, but as recently as yesterday that hadn't appeared to be in the cards anytime soon.

But yesterday, Jared hadn't been thinking about that vendetta. Wending his way over narrow, unpaved roads, he'd driven through dusk and into darkness, mulling over the decision he must make. He was at a crossroads and he knew it, for he'd been offered a ton of money for Wolf Cache Systems.

Day or night, he knew the way by heart, every tree and bump and ridge, every road and trail and cabin. As always, his heart lifted as he drove across the narrow stream flowing at the foot of the clearing before the cabin, a darker shadow set against a backdrop of trees. For a few minutes he sat in the car with the windows wide, just breathing the sweet air of home and letting his eyes grow accustomed to the darkness.

And something else. Something sweet and... feminine.

Every muscle tensed. Slowly, soundlessly, he'd stepped from the vehicle.

Something hadn't been right. He had no idea what set off alarm bells in his mind but they were definitely clanging. He'd stopped by just a couple of days earlier to begin restocking for the summer, and he knew; something inexplicable had changed.

And then he'd found out what—and knew that at last, his patience had been rewarded.

Jared walked back inside the cabin as unexpectedly as he'd walked out forty-five minutes earlier. Lark, in the process of sweeping the floor, started at his sudden appearance.

Standing there with the light streaming through the doorway behind him, he looked like...like a mythical hero, she thought in awe. He wore hiking boots this morning, denim trousers and a plaid shirt. He looked every inch a man to match this wild and beautiful land.

He crossed the room with easy strides, stopping before her to look deeply into her eyes. She held her breath but refused to turn away, sensing that if she did his next words would be of dismissal. Instead she lifted her chin and stared right back at him, determined not to show the trepidation she felt.

"Here's the deal," he said, clipping off the words. "You can stay temporarily but only if we get a few things straight."

"Such as?"

His eyes flickered with what looked like satisfaction. "Our roles will be reversed, for starters."

"Our roles?" She frowned. "What in the world does that mean?"

"It means that I'm in charge and you who must please. You'll take care of the cabin, do the cooking and cleaning and anything else I tell you to do."

"*Anything*?" *Anything* covered a lot of territory...territory she thought of every time she looked at him. It was ridiculous to keep remembering a childish crush but when he said things like that—

He smiled, and she promptly forgot not only what she'd said but what she'd been thinking.

"Anything. You won't have any complaints. Trust me."

"You have got to be kidding," she said faintly. "If...if I don't please you, will you just throw me out the door?"

"No, sweetheart. If you don't please me, I'll call Daddy."

Her stomach knotted at his threat—or was it a promise?—and at the sudden heat she saw in his eyes. Here was a very, very dangerous man and she was about to put herself deliberately beneath his power. But what was the alternative? Crawling back to Florida like a—

"Yes," she said in a determined voice. "Yes, I'll please you. I know you think I'm a total airhead but I can cook—I actually enjoy it—and clean and whatever else needs doing around here. And I won't intrude on your time or space, because I came here for solitude myself. Deal?''

Impulsively, she thrust out her hand. For a moment he looked at it, finally reaching out to envelope it in his own. His skin felt warm and dry, but rough, as a working man's would. A little thrill of excitement shot up her arm, reminding her of the times she'd hit her crazy bone and been practically paralyzed.

She licked her lips. ''Will you answer one question?''

''Maybe.''

Why didn't he release her hand? The numbness seemed to be spreading... ''Why do you hate me?'' she blurted. ''I thought we were friends, once. What did I ever do—?''

But she was talking to thin air.

Confused and unhappy, she leaned against her broom and tried to figure out what he might have against her. Whatever it was, it had happened a long time ago.

He'd been a quiet boy then, a hardworking boy. He'd done everything he'd been told to do, competently and without complaint: run errands, chop wood, make cabin repairs, even cut back brush and foliage to enlarge the clearing around the house— most of which, she noted, had been allowed to re-establish itself and reclaim the land.

She thought he'd liked her best then, and it hurt to think she'd been wrong. He'd treated all of them in a rather distant manner, but with her, she'd always thought there was... if not an underlayer of affection, at least of favor.

She had followed him around, when he'd allow it, which wasn't often. Risa had flirted with him shamelessly; their mother had ignored him; and their father...

Well, Drake Mallory hadn't treated Jared any differently than he treated the rest of his underlings, Lark thought defensively. Her father spit out brusque orders, showed a complete lack of sensitivity to the feelings of others, and on the rare occasions when Jared balked at a command, turned nasty and insulting until he got his way, which he always did.

Why had Jared taken such abuse? she wondered for the first time. As a child, she'd supposed it hadn't bothered him all that much or he wouldn't have kept coming back for more. Now, that no longer seemed possible.

Jared Wolf was a proud man and he'd been a proud boy. He couldn't have stayed on for the money, which she was sure had been a pittance for the work he did— not only what he was told, but much, much more.

And perhaps therein lay a clue. Could he have stayed for love of this place when money wasn't enough?

This time Jared walked through the forest all the way to the hot springs almost two miles distant. Once there, he slid down onto a boulder and watched water tumble over a small waterfall and into the pool below.

A smile twitched at his lips. *Payback time*, he thought with relish; payback time!

If revenge was the cake, then Lark Mallory would be the frosting ... and dessert had been a long time coming.

CHAPTER THREE

LARK had every intention of fulfilling her part of the bargain. Further speculation about Jared's motives wouldn't get her anywhere, so she set to work sweeping, scrubbing, cleaning everything in sight. If Jared thought she was some kind of hothouse flower, he was quite mistaken. She'd learned a lot during those two years in Miami with her mother—

No, she wouldn't think about that. She'd also learned a lot the few months she'd spent living on her own. She'd been happy in her tiny apartment until her father suffered a mild heart attack, which sent her running back to the mansion on Jupiter Island.

At the time, she'd rationalized that she'd let her mother down; she couldn't fail her father, too. She already carried enough guilt to last a lifetime, so she'd come crawling back at her father's command.

Now she worked willingly, determined to do her duty and fulfill her benefactor's expectations.

At noon, she put a lunch of canned soup and cheese sandwiches on the table and sat down to wait for him. And wait. By the time he appeared, the soup was cold and the bread on the sandwiches dry and hard, but she forgot all that when she saw him stride across the kitchen to drop three sleek and shiny fish into a pan.

"Rainbow trout," he announced with satisfaction. "Make a good supper."

Looking at Jared, then at his catch, the funniest feeling stole over Lark. He was the hunter providing for his mate, and there was something both primitive and exciting about that concept.

She nodded. "I've never cleaned a fish," she said faintly.

"You'll never learn any younger." His lips tilted with amusement. He looked at the table, without the slightest indication of either approval or disapproval. "Cold soup?"

"It was hot earlier." She nodded toward the cook stove. "I managed a small fire—not a good one, but it did the job. If you're willing to wait a few minutes, I can just—"

She reached for the bowls, intent upon returning the contents to the pot for re-heating, but he stopped her by wrapping one hand around her slender wrist. She froze, her alarmed gaze flying to his face.

"Don't bother," he said.

"It's no bother," she whispered.

"Stoking up a wood fire?" He raised one brow, tilting his head to look into her face. "Sit down and we'll eat."

She did, hiding her confusion by dropping her napkin into her lap and reaching for the glass of sun tea, diluted by melting ice cubes. She sipped, watching him from beneath lowered lashes.

Feeling a need to make conversation, she cast about for a safe subject. "There've been a lot of changes in the cabin since the last time I was here," she observed.

His dark eyes narrowed. "I've been putting it back the way it was, the way it was always supposed to be. Your father—" He broke off abruptly, his expression thoughtful. "Your father was the one who changed it. Took out all the original furniture, dumped it into a shed where the elements could take their toll, brought in electricity and modern plumbing—''

''I'm sorry,'' Lark apologized for her father, although she wasn't at all sure why electricity and modern plumbing would be considered ''bad.''

Jared obviously saw right through her, for he said, ''You don't have a clue what I'm mad about, do you?''

''Well . . . No.'' She busied herself making crumbs of her bread crust. ''I mean, most people would call those things improvements.''

''Maybe I can explain it to you.'' He dropped a half-eaten sandwich back on the plate. ''Or maybe I can't. Maybe our values are too different.'' He looked at her with brooding disapproval.

His condemnation stung but she kept her face impassive, refusing to defend herself or her values. After a moment, he leaned back in his chair and went on.

''Wolf Cabin . . . is my family's homeplace, our birthright. Getting it back from that bast—from Drake Mallory gave me more satisfaction than just about anything I've ever done.''

She sensed a wealth of emotion in him. ''Then this place has been in your family for a long time?'' she asked gently.

''My great-grandfather built this cabin with his own hands, along about 1900. He did it for my great-grandmother, and they lived the rest of their lives here. He also made most of the furniture tossed out like so much junk.''

Lark shivered. ''This must have been true wilderness almost a century ago.''

His mouth curved up in a sardonic line. ''You mean even more so than it is now? Yes, but that's one of the reasons he chose Wolf's Head Pass. Hell, he was Ute Indian and she was Irish. Isolation must have had a certain appeal."

She looked at him blankly, the implication of what he'd just said sinking in but slowly. "You mean back then it wasn't...?" Her voice trailed off in confusion, for she was unsure how to say it without offering fresh offense

He gave a bitter laugh. "Back then?" He crossed his arms over his broad chest in a belligerent gesture. "No one in the family ever spoke of it but it couldn't have been easy for an Indian and a white woman."

Picking up his soup spoon, he began to eat again. She waited, and when he failed to go on with the story, ventured a question.

"So what happened?"

He shrugged. "What happened? The same thing that happened to their children and their children's children—they lived happily ever after. I come from a long line of happy, if slightly peculiar, marriages. I've got Indian, Irish, Mexican, German and English in me, and that's just what I know of for sure. But I'm proud as hell of every bit of it."

Looking at him with awe and admiration, Lark fancied that she could see every heritage of which he spoke. Each had contributed the best of which it was capable to create this incredible man. "Tell me more about your family...please?"

"I've already told you too much. Let's cut the idle chitchat and get down to brass tacks."

"B-brass tacks?"

"You're hiding out from your father, right?"

She licked suddenly dry lips and nodded.

"If you don't want him to find you, you'd better get that rental car back to the agency in a big hurry."

"Why? I paid cash," she objected.

"They didn't take driver's license information and a credit card for backup?"

"Well, yes, but—"

"But nothing. If your father's hot on your trail, he'll track you there and extort the information he needs. Once he figures out that you're on the loose in Colorado, where will he look first?"

Her heart sank. "You're right, but I have to have transportation. What should I do?"

"Return the car tomorrow and 'accidentally' let slip information to mislead your father, if he or his minions come snooping around. I'll follow in the Land Rover and bring you back here."

"But that would mean—" That would mean she'd be totally dependent upon him, not even capable of coming or going on her own.

"That would mean," he echoed softly, "that you'd be completely in my power... at my mercy. Does that possibility frighten you, Lark Mallory?"

She lifted her chin and looked him in the eye. "No," she said firmly, and it was the truth. The thought of being in his power and at his mercy didn't frighten her in the slightest.

Instead she found it strangely exciting—which realization frightened her very much indeed.

He proclaimed her first foray into fish cookery a success. In all fairness she had to admit he'd helped by cleaning his catch, something she'd been less than eager to attempt. After they ate, he disappeared again—something he did frequently, she was learning—while she cleaned up the kitchen.

She was rapidly learning her way around the cabin. Although he'd done a lot to return it to its former primitive state, he'd kept the water system her father had installed, and the power generator to run the small, old-fashioned refrigerator. But no electric lights were in evidence; heating or cooking were handled by two fireplaces and the wood cook stove.

She found something wildly romantic and ageless about log cabins in general, but especially one nestled at the top of a wooded mountain pass in a flower meadow with a running stream below. Hanging up her dish towel, she wandered out back onto the wooden deck—more of her father's handiwork, but apparently Jared hadn't been able to resist the view, either.

The beauty of the mountains stunned her. She caught her breath and laid her hands on the wooden railing, feeling a deep sense of peace and contentment permeate her body and spirit.

She had been right to come here.

"The Indians called them the Shining Mountains."

His bemused tone made her jump with surprise and dig her fingernails into the wood. "I can see why," she murmured.

"Is the altitude bothering you? We're something like 10,000 feet above sea level here. That's enough to throw some people, until they get used to it."

"No problems." Squaring her shoulders, she turned to face him, leaning back against hands braced on the railing. "I'm a little short of breath, but I remember that from when we used to come here before."

He nodded. It was getting close to nine o'clock and nearly dark, so he was little more than a substantial shadow. Yet she felt the power of his presence as if he stood in a spotlight.

"Be sure to drink plenty of water and don't push yourself too hard for the next few days," he advised. "No headaches?"

"No."

"Good girl. You must be tougher than you look."

How to respond to that? Praise counterbalanced by the insulting "girl," then practically being told she looked like a wimp? Before she could think of a way to respond, he crossed to stand beside her.

His sigh sounded like pure satisfaction. "This really is a helluva view, even at night."

"Yes. But I have to admit, it's making a much greater impression on me now than it did all those years ago. I can't believe how little I *learned*, how little I remember."

"Such as?"

"Oh, about the plants and animals, the names of the mountains, that sort of thing. All I know is Pikes Peak, and everyone knows that."

"Unfortunately, much of what 'everyone' knows is wrong. The Peak is great but it's far from being Colorado's most impressive mountain—or even the tallest."

"No! You mean—?"

"Yep. Thirty mountains in Colorado are taller. The Peak's the tallest on the Front Range, though, so it was the one the pioneers saw as they approached the Rockies."

They stood for a few minutes in an increasingly intimate silence. He was the first to speak.

"Over there," he pointed toward jagged shadows to the southwest, "is the Sangre de Cristo Range. The story goes that a Spanish priest saw a blood-red sunset over the peaks and cried, '*Sangre de Cristo!*'"

"Blood of Christ," she translated.

"That's right. The name stuck. Mountain names came about all kinds of ways. There's Mount Shavano in the Sawatches, named for a leader of the Mountain Utes, and there's Teddy Peak in the Culebras—"

"Named for Teddy bears?"

"Close but no cigar. Named for Teddy Roosevelt."

The light had faded completely while they talked. A rustle of sound warned her he was moving. She tensed, half expecting...what? Not the opening of the door, certainly, or the scratch of a match as he lit a kerosene lamp. Apparently the impromptu geography lesson was over, she realized with regret.

"It's about time we cleared out a space in the second bedroom where you can sleep," his deep voice suggested from within. "Or if you prefer, you can always bunk on the floor again or...with me."

She was glad of the darkness for it hid the fiery glow scorching her cheeks. "I'll take the second bedroom, thank you very much." She joined him in the kitchen, where he waited to lead the way.

Leading seemed to be something he did quite naturally, she realized with sinking heart.

They set out for Colorado Springs right after breakfast the next morning, Jared leading the way in his Land Rover. Lark found it necessary to concentrate on her driving in order to keep up with him, which meant she missed some of the most spectacular scenery in the Rockies.

She'd missed most of it when she arrived, too, having to concentrate then on finding the way, then dealing with growing darkness as the sun settled over the western mountains. At least she should be able to enjoy the sights on the return trip, for Jared would be in the driver's seat.

As if he wasn't now. She shivered.

At the small airport on the southeast edge of Colorado Springs, Jared hung back while Lark returned the car. When the friendly attendant inquired about the success of her visit, she remembered Jared's suggestion and blithely declared her trip a delight, adding that she hoped to enjoy Albuquerque just as much.

With that she sailed away across the street and into the airport terminal, where she turned right and walked the length of the building before exiting. Jared's Land Rover idled near the curb and she jumped in, hunching down so she wouldn't be seen.

"I gave 'em the slip," she cried happily, laughing up at him. "Let's make our getaway!"

And they did. Whether it would be good enough to fool her father, only time would tell.

Once back on the street, Lark sat up and looked around with interest while Jared turned the Land Rover west, toward the mountains dominated by stately Pikes Peak. Through Old Colorado City he drove, with its bungalows and charming Victorians, then on to Manitou Springs, nestled at the very foot of Colorado's Front Range.

Lark sighed wistfully, watching the Buffalo Bill Wax Museum flash past, then the shops and the town clock and the signs announcing the sites of Manitou's famous mineral springs. "We—Risa and I—always used to beg Father to stop and let us look around here but he never would," she said as they exited on the western side of town and started up the steep grade leading into the mountains.

Jared gave her an incredulous glance. "You mean all those years your family came through here, he never stopped?"

"Never once. We'd go straight to the cabin and that's where we'd stay until time to go home again. Then we'd go straight through to the airport again and leave. I wasn't kidding when I told you I know almost nothing about the area, or the state for that matter."

"Tourists." It sounded like a dirty word, the way he said it. "Okay, we're going up Ute Pass. You get caught in here during a blizzard, winds howling down, and it can be a real nightmare."

She could see why. The steep highway seemed to have been cut through solid red rock. Looking up, up...her sense of the familiar everyday world seemed to fall away with every foot they ascended.

They passed several bikers pumping like crazy; Colorado was big biking country, even she knew that. Pines and scrub oak began to dot the hillsides and at last they emerged atop the pass. Only a few more miles and they entered the town of Woodland Park. A sign declared the elevation to be 8,465 feet.

"Why do they put altitude instead of population on city limit signs in Colorado?" she wondered aloud.

Jared shrugged. "Officially? Who knows? My guess is that most Coloradans are like me—they don't consider population a plus. Altitude, on the other hand, is something to brag about."

On the far edge of town, they passed a sign that made Lark smile: a drawing of a donkey and an old prospector pointing the way, and a legend which she read aloud: "'Yonder lies Cripple Creek.'"

"That's where we're headed," Jared said, not taking his attention off the two-lane road. "Need to pick up a few supplies, since I've got an extra mouth to feed." He shot her an assessing glance. "Skinny as you are, that shouldn't take much."

Lark flashed back on her wedding consultant's complaint and Risa's defense which she resurrected now. "A woman can never be too rich or too thin," she declared.

"The hell she can't. I like a woman with a little meat on her bones." Again that measuring glance, as if he were deliberately trying to goad her into an argument.

Well, let him try. Lark hated any kind of altercation and refused to become embroiled in one. Fighting was not her style; the only time she'd ever really tried had been a disaster.

"To each his own," she said loftily, but she thought she caught a flash of disappointment on his face just before she turned her attention to the glorious scenery gliding past. He must think her completely without spirit, she brooded. Living with a world-class fighter like her father had pretty much knocked all the fight out of her.

She spoke calmly, as if Jared's poor opinion of her didn't sting at all. "I could use a few things, too, if there's time to do a little shopping. I left Florida with just the clothes on my back. I bought a couple of T-shirts and a pair of hiking boots in Colorado Springs before I drove up to the cabin, but that's about it. I don't even have a bathing suit."

"Don't buy one on my account," he said. "Until you've skinny-dipped in a hot spring, you haven't lived."

She could imagine . . . closing her eyes to savor the pleasure of slipping beneath the warm and silky waters without a stitch on, then opening her eyes to find Jared Wolf there before her . . . waiting, just as in her youthful fantasies.

She made a little choking sound and sat up straight. Another sign flashed past. "This is God's country so don't drive through it like hell." A smile was just what she needed.

And then she saw another sight not common to Florida: a herd of deer—or maybe elk, she wasn't sure—grazing peacefully alongside several horses in a meadow.

An amazing country, Colorado, she thought, stealing a glance at her companion and appreciating his strong, stark profile.

A strange country that bred wondrous sights . . . and powerful men.

Lark had been to Cripple Creek once before, but that was many years ago when it was nothing more than a sleepy little town with a scarlet past and not much of a future. When the Land Rover turned down the main street of the "World's Greatest Gold Camp," she gasped in astonishment.

"What in the world has happened here?" she wondered aloud.

"Some call it progress." Jared's tone made it clear that wasn't what *he* would call it. "Low stakes gambling was approved a few years back and it started another boom. I try to ignore it.''

Lots of luck, she thought, taking in the construction and renovation under way on both sides of Bennett Avenue. Obviously, some pains were being taken to protect the town's past glory, for to Lark, the community looked as if it had dropped out of the pages of a history book.

Jared steered the Land Rover to the right, onto a dirt road leading up the hillside. Lark glanced at him in surprise but he made no explanation for turning away from the business section.

Past log houses, he drove; past house trailers set up on foundations, cottages and a school. Finally he pulled into a driveway before a neat frame house and killed the engine.

Curiosity got the better of her. "Who lives here?" she asked. "A friend of yours?"

"You could say that." He opened his door. "My sister and nephew—"

Anything else he might have intended to say was lost in a whoop of delight issuing from a small boy who'd appeared on the porch. "On-too Jurd, On-too Jurd," the child shouted, holding out his pudgy arms and jumping up and down.

He was the most adorable child Lark had ever seen, even if he hadn't mastered the verbal mechanics of "Uncle Jared." One glance and she was lost.

"My goodness," Jenny Wolf said. "My goodness, this is such a surprise."

Jenny and Lark sat on rocking chairs on Jenny's front porch, glasses of lemonade resting on a table between them, while Jared hauled Little Jared around and around the house in a wagon. Lark was entirely enchanted with the scene—more so because Jared's gentleness with the child astonished her. Would he be equally gentle with a woman...?

Lark pulled her imagination up short. "I'm as surprised as you are," she told Jared's beautiful sister. "I didn't even know my father had sold the cabin or of course I wouldn't have shown up out of the blue."

"Why *did* you?"

Lark was beginning to like this outspoken young woman a great deal, even when she asked hard questions. "I have some...personal decisions to make. I needed time and space to do that in and I remembered the cabin, and how happy I'd been there."

Jenny nodded. "Makes perfect sense to me." She added with a smile, "Must have been a shock, running into Jared."

"Yes." An understatement. "But he's kindly consented to let me stay, which I greatly appreciate. You see..." She bit her lip. "I didn't tell my father where I was going, since he's part of the problem I'm wrestling with. If Jared hadn't taken me in, I don't know where I could have gone."

Jenny's blue eyes flew wide. "But of course he'd take you in! Jared's not the kind of man who'd toss a woman out on her fanny on top of a mountain!" Laughing, she picked up her lemonade glass and sipped.

Lark wasn't convinced but she didn't argue the point. "Jenny, may I ask a favor of you?"

"Ask away." Jenny's expression remained open and friendly, without the faintest shadow.

"I'd like to call my sister in Florida to tell her I'm all right. I'll put it on my credit card."

"Of course. The telephone is just inside the door."
Jenny stood up. "Take your time. I'll just go check
on my child."

Lark watched Jenny skip off the porch and launch
a surprise attack on her son and brother. Soon the
three of them were wrestling around on the soft, green
grass.

With envy so sharp and unexpected it made her feel
almost ill, Lark turned away to make her call.

"Risa, Risa, it's me—no, don't say my name!"

"Lark! Thank God. Don't worry, I'm alone."

Lark let out her breath with relief. "Good. How's
everything back there?"

"Are you kidding? Father is still in an absolute rage,
although he's pretending—"

"Pretending what?"

"That you've gone to a health spa in California to
get ready for the wedding." She hesitated. "Uhhh...is
there going to *be* a wedding?"

"I don't know. I—I haven't had time to think about
it much."

"You haven't had time to think about it! You've
been gone for days and days. What have you been
doing?"

What, indeed? Meeting a mysterious and handsome
man, cleaning for him, cooking for him, chatting with
his sister, admiring his nephew— "No time to go into
all that," Lark said hurriedly. "I just wanted to let
you know I'm fine."

"OK, Lark, this has gone far enough. Tell me where
you are."

"Now, Risa, we agreed that for your
own sake—"

"But that was before I realized you wouldn't be back in a day or two. Now I want to know—immediately!"

"I'm sorry but I can't tell you. Father would get it out of you one way or the other."

"But what if something happened to you? What if you got sick, or hurt yourself? How would we find out?"

"I'm not going to get sick or hurt myself, all right? But if I did, I—" She broke off just in time, before she could say, *I'm with people who'd see I was taken care of,* and substituted, "I do have identification."

"But this has gotten entirely out of hand. The wedding is only a few weeks away and—"

"And that's plenty of time. Look, I can't talk any longer. Just don't worry. I'll call when I can."

She hung up and stood for a moment, head down and body trembling. It wasn't until she'd walked back out onto the porch several minutes later that she realized she hadn't even asked about Wes, not to mention her car and engagement ring.

They arrived back at Wolf Cabin in late afternoon. Jared pulled around to the back and parked the Land Rover, then jumped out to unload the supplies they'd picked up at the Mountain Mom 'n' Pop Store.

Lark followed more slowly. After a big lunch at one of Cripple Creek's many casinos before heading out, she still felt pleasantly replete and more than a little drowsy.

But she should help with the unloading; that was, after all, part of her job. Grabbing several packages, she started up the back steps, meeting Jared on his way down for a second load.

"I'll get the rest," he said.

"No, let me. It's my job."

"The hell it is. Give me those. I'm not going to let a woman—"

She recoiled from his reaching hands. "I've got them. Just—"

Trying to back up the stairs to evade him, she felt one heel slip off a step. Packages flew out of her arms. There was no time to grab the rail for support, or do anything else to avoid a tumble down the stairs—

And right into Jared Wolf's hard body. She found herself pressed against a chest that felt like granite, held there by arms like steel bands, and looking up into the startled face of her savior.

And then it wasn't surprise she saw but a swift realization that she really *was* in his arms.

"Well, well, well," he said in a cat's satisfied purr— and kissed her.

She'd expected—or perhaps the word was *hoped*— this would happen sooner or later, but she'd never dreamed it would be so powerful when it did. *Anything*, he'd said; she must do anything he asked of her. But he wouldn't ask too much! Of course not... even if she kissed him back, even if she curled her arms around his neck and—

She turned her head aside, breaking the kiss, gasping for breath. Her heart felt as if it would pound right on through the barrier of her chest, so painfully did it throb. Her lips tingled from contact with his and she feared that if he stood her on her own two legs, she'd topple right on over.

Regaining enough breath to move, she pushed feebly at his chest. He ignored her fluttering hands to shower tiny kisses on her cheek, her throat, holding her a prisoner in his embrace with no more effort than it would take to restrain a wild bird.

When he reached for her lips again, she found the strength to say what she should have said in the first place. "Stop! Please, stop!"

He nuzzled her cheek. "Give me one good reason why I should, Goldilocks."

Reason? She could give him a dozen but only one was a *good* reason. "Because," she cried, *"I'm engaged!"*

Even braced for the worst, she wasn't prepared for his reaction.

CHAPTER FOUR

"YOU'RE *what*?"

Jared stood her on her feet with so much force he almost rattled her teeth. Groping blindly for a banister, she managed to remain upright, but just barely. Nothing like this had ever happened to her before; he'd kissed her until her knees went weak.

Why was he staring at her that way? Her mind seemed to have gone perfectly blank.

His dark eyes narrowed even further and he spoke from between gritted teeth. "Did you say you're engaged?"

"W-well, yes..."

"You took your own sweet time telling me."

"It didn't seem pertinent." Oh, dear. That hadn't come out at all like she'd intended. "I mean, of course it was pertinent to *me*, but it didn't seem pertinent in relationship to you." She bit her lip in consternation. "How was I to know—?" How was she to know his kiss would turn her world upside down?

"How were you to know you'd tangle with a man who still believes marriage is sacred?" he demanded. "And a man's word is sacred, too, if he's any kind of man. What's a *woman's* word worth, Lark Mallory?"

She caught her breath on a little gasp. "You don't understand. I came here to—"

"It's too late for your rationalizations. An engaged woman doesn't do what you've done, act like you've

been acting, if she respects the promise she's made."
His scorn lashed at her. "I'm grateful for one thing,
though."

She knew she shouldn't ask, but couldn't help
herself. "W-what's that?"

"This will make it a hell of a lot easier for me to
do what needs to be done."

She stood there numbly while he vaulted to the
ground and headed toward the timberline at an easy
lope. She was beginning to understand that about him;
when he was angry or agitated he would disappear
into the wilderness to emerge hours later with a new
serenity.

How she envied him that. With heavy heart, she
picked up her fallen packages and turned to enter the
cabin. What had he meant when he spoke of "what
needs to be done"? Probably just that from now on,
he'd keep his distance, she decided.

Should she have told him about her engagement
earlier? She didn't see why, since it didn't concern him
in the slightest... until he kissed her. True, an engaged woman shouldn't go around kissing other men,
but Lark hadn't initiated that cataclysmic occurrence.

She touched her lips lightly with her fingertips,
fancying that she could still feel the imprint of his
mouth there. In all honesty, could she say she had not
yearned to know how it would feel to be in his arms,
to know his kiss? Maybe he was right; maybe she had
been in some way unfaithful to her promise to Wes.

Maybe Jared Wolf was right to despise her.

Jared returned long after dark. Lark, sitting on the
deck out back with a light quilt wrapped around her

shoulders to ward off mountain chill, persistent even in July, rose at his approach.

"I kept dinner for you," she said anxiously. "It'll only take me a minute to—"

"Never mind." He brushed past her, a darker shadow in the night. "I've eaten."

What and where, she couldn't imagine, but didn't want to offend him further by asking. "I also wanted to apologize for what happened earlier," she forced herself to add as she hurried into the cabin after him.

He turned, the fluid motion illuminated by the kerosene lamp. "Apologizing for the kiss or for lying to your fiancé?"

"I never lied to my fiancé," she cried, aghast.

"No? He knows you're here, then, and approves."

"Not...exactly." She hugged the quilt more tightly around her.

His dark eyebrows soared. "You mean he wouldn't look with favor on your current living arrangements?"

"My—?"

"Are you or are you not living with another man in the middle of nowhere?"

"There's 'living with' and there's *living with*. You and I both know there's nothing going on between us."

"Wrong." There was something dark and wicked about the look he gave her. "Past tense—nothing *was* going on between us, nothing overt, at any rate. Now that's all changed."

She shook her head. "You're wrong. Now that you know everything, surely you'll—"

"But *do* I know everything?" He took a menacing step toward her, reaching out to tangle the fingers of one hand in the red-gold curls tumbling around her shoulders. "I have a sneaking suspicion that the answer to that is 'no.' If my hunch is correct, all bets are off."

"W-what do you mean?" She could barely speak, couldn't move at all beneath the faint stroking of his hand against the side of her neck, beneath her hair.

"As long as you're engaged, you're safe from me . . . mostly. I don't mess with other men's women. But if the runaway bride has no intention of honoring her pledge, that's a whole other story."

His gaze held her captive while his touch mesmerized her. She stared at him with slightly parted lips, breathless and dazed. She'd come here to make up her mind about her future and instead found herself mired more deeply in indecision than when she'd arrived.

So her answer was *no*, she hadn't decided to end her engagement. If she made that choice now and said so, Jared might pick her up and carry her to his bed, where she would more than likely be incinerated by his flame.

She was no match for this man! Jared Wolf required a woman of fire and spirit, not some cowardly individual who'd always been a daughter first, her own woman second, if at all.

He leaned closer and she felt the warmth of his breath on her cheek when he spoke in taunting, tantalizing tones. "So are you still engaged to be married . . . in your heart as well as in fact?"

"Yes. . . ." She drew the single word out on a soft moan.

His hand fell away. "When that situation changes— and it will, let me know."

He left her there alone in the kitchen, sagging weakly against the corner of the table.

Time passed with agonizing slowness. Although Jared treated her with cool courtesy, Lark knew that everything had changed between them. Beneath his imperturbable exterior lurked the predator for which he was named. For her part, she felt no more able to defend herself, should he choose to spring, than the small, drab lark she saw outside the cabin window three days later.

This was getting her nowhere. She leaned her forehead against the glass pane, reminding herself why she'd come here: to decide whether she could go through with her wedding. But instead of thinking about that, about her relationships with her father and her fiancé, she found almost her every waking hour centering around the object of her puppy love more than a decade earlier.

She wasn't going to be able to hide out here forever, she reminded herself. Her father would eventually find her, or Jared Wolf would get tired of his cat-and-mouse game and throw her out.

And in any event, she had to make up her mind in time to return for the wedding—either to cancel it or go through with it.

I'll make up my mind today, she decided. Jared had wandered off somewhere, as he often did, so there was no reason she couldn't do likewise. In fact . . . she smiled with anticipated pleasure. She'd see if she could find the hot springs back in the forest, where she and Risa used to frolic as kids. There'd been a path, she recalled, so all she had to do was find it. Of course, she didn't have a swimsuit but that wouldn't matter, since she'd be alone.

Excited at the prospect of an innocent adventure, she let herself out the front door and walked quickly up the slope into the aspen grove. By the time she got there, she was already breathing hard. Although she'd never suffered from true altitude sickness, she did find herself tiring more easily and breathing more heavily.

Small price to pay for air as pure and sweet as this, she told herself, turning at the edge of the trees to look out over the pass below. *I'm on top of the world*, she exulted. *I'm free!* Suddenly she felt wonderful.

Turning, she plunged between the trees, trying to find the trail. But everything was different. This stand of aspens hadn't even been here, or its undergrowth of wildflowers. What had happened to the evergreens?

A cloud of blue columbines beckoned and she dropped to her knees to touch a brilliant bloom with reverent fingers. Before, she'd picked huge bouquets of wildflowers to present to her mother, hoping to bring a smile to a woman too rarely happy. Now, as an adult, she wouldn't dream of disturbing the environment any more than was required by her careful passage.

Slowly she wandered through the aspen grove, enjoying the rattle of a gentle breeze among the leaves, the scurry of tiny furry creatures in the undergrowth. A rabbit darted almost from beneath her feet; a falcon circled lazily overhead.

But still she didn't allow troublesome thoughts to intrude, merely drinking in the sights and sounds of the high country. Enchanted, she turned first this way, then that, seeking the trail she felt sure was just beyond the next ridge, just past the next boulder, just around the next bend.

And so when she finally struck a faint but definite path through the pine, the fir, the spruce, she quickened her pace to skip along it happily. It wasn't far now. She could hardly wait to—

Rounding a bend in the trail, she plowed into Jared Wolf's hard chest. Bracing her palms against him, she pushed away in alarm. He let her go, never once raising his hands to either help or hinder.

"Jared!" she exclaimed. "You scared me!"

"Good." His frown didn't lighten. He crossed his arms over his chest, his biceps bulging beneath the short sleeves of his T-shirt, and thrust out his jaw at a belligerent angle. "Where the hell do you think you're going?"

"To the hot springs, if that's any concern of yours," she said, hurt by his attitude. He had no reason to treat her like a wayward child.

"No, you're not."

"I am so and you can't stop me." Deliberately, she stepped off the trail, walked around him, then turned back. "See? I'm going."

"Fine." The solid jaw jutted out even further. "You're going—but not to the hot springs."

"I am, Jared." She sounded almost pleading, even to herself.

"No, you're not," he insisted with exaggerated patience. "You're going to Lookout Point. That is, you are if you don't fall off a mountain or get lost in the deep, dark woods first. The hot spring is over there." He waved vaguely to her left. "You're on the wrong trail, Goldilocks."

"Oh." Crestfallen, she stared at the toes of her hiking boots, dirty and stained with earth and grass.

"Jeez," he said, his irritation surging to the fore. "Don't you know a tenderfoot can get killed wandering around in the forest alone?" Reaching out, he grabbed her arm and shoved her a few steps back the way she'd come. "There are animals out here, including bears and cats—"

As he spoke, he pushed her along before him. Emerging from the trees, he stopped short. Pointing to a muddy patch next to the trail, he demanded, "See that?"

She followed his pointing finger. All she saw was a muddy hodgepodge of tracks in the mud.

He knelt with his usual graceful economy, his iron grip forcing her down beside him. With his other hand, he lightly touched a series of ridges and indentations. "Cat," he said.

"Cat?" She peered more closely. "Away out here?"

He looked at her as if she'd lost her mind. "Wildcat. Bobcat. Cougar."

"Wildcat!" She jumped to her feet, heart pounding, her anxious gaze swinging around the small meadow. "Where is it?"

"Gone, I hope to hell. Now do you see why I can't let you wander around out here by yourself? God only knows what you might bump into—or what might bump into you. How would I explain that to Mr. Right?"

"Don't call him that!" Keeping up with his long strides wasn't easy, even with him pulling her along. "He has a name."

"Yeah? If he does, you've never mentioned it to me."

"Oh." She probably hadn't, at that. "His name is Wes. Wesley Sherborn, to be precise."

"Wesley." They were entering the aspen stand and he pulled her around in front of him on the path. "Yeah, you look like the kind of girl who'd get involved with a Wesley."

She knew that was an insult but she wasn't quite sure how; in any event, she preferred to ignore such jibes. "What I don't understand," she gasped, out of breath from their headlong retreat, "is why it's so dangerous now, when Risa and I used to wander alone all over the place."

"You were smarter then. And you weren't alone."

"Of course we were."

"I was always around."

"You? But—"

"I was looking out for you, okay? Let it drop. I—"

They'd just emerged on the ridge above the cabin. Following his gaze, Lark saw the mini-van parked before the cabin and she cried out in alarm; *her father had found her!* Whirling to grab Jared's forearm in supplication, she saw him smile.

"Jenny's here," he said, his pleasure evident.

Shaking off her grasp, he started down the slope alone.

The change in Jared was mind-boggling to Lark. One minute he'd been dragging her through the wilderness giving her holy hell and the next he was cooing and making goo-goo eyes at Little Jared.

She sighed.

Jenny, swirling ice cubes in a glass of sun tea, gave her companion a quizzical glance. "How you two been getting along?" she asked too casually.

"Guess." Lark laughed ruefully. "Jenny..." Lark looked out over the emerald landscape. "Why does Jared dislike me so?"

"Does he?" Jenny looked honestly surprised. "If that's the case, I have no idea why. Your father, on the other hand..." She shook her head wryly.

"He's said a little about that but his attitude seems all out of proportion," Lark mused. "I mean, my father's not the most lovable man in the world—"

Jenny snorted indelicately.

Lark laughed. "All right, he's arrogant and overbearing and I've spent my entire life trying to please him and failing more often than not. But what could he possibly have done to make Jared despise him so?"

Jenny looked suddenly serious. "Not just to Jared. To the entire Wolf clan. I probably shouldn't get into it—" She glanced toward her brother, engrossed with her son in a minute examination of a pinecone.

Lark shifted uneasily. "That's all right, then. I wouldn't want you to—"

"I probably shouldn't but I will," Jenny interrupted with a laugh. "You don't think I'd let Jared intimidate me, do you?"

"He intimidates me," Lark admitted. "Without even trying, I'm afraid."

"Hey, in my family, you learn to fight back because if you don't, you'll get trampled," Jenny said cheerfully. "Besides, his bark is lots worse than his bite."

"Maybe."

"You don't look convinced. But never mind that. You asked about my family's feelings for your father." She took a sip of tea before going on. "Basically, your father stole this cabin."

Lark gave a nervous little laugh. "Wow, you really don't mince words, do you?"

"Not unless I have to. You wouldn't have asked if you didn't want the truth, right? What happened was, a year after our father died, your father approached our mother saying he wanted to buy this place for a summer retreat. Jared was...about thirteen at the time, and I was only four or five."

Lark frowned. "But that can't be right. How old are you now, Jenny?"

"Twenty-three. Jared is thirty-one. Why?"

"Well, I'm twenty-six, three years older than you are. And I distinctly remember, I was eleven when Father bought this place."

"Are you remembering when he bought it, or the first time you came here?"

"Why... What are you trying to say?"

"That Mr. Mallory owned this place several years before he brought his family here. I guess he used it for..." another furtive glance in the direction of her brother "...business."

"What kind of business?"

"Private business—who knows? Anyway, getting back to the story, no one in my family had actually lived here for several years—it was too small, really—although my father and Jared took care of it. We were living on a bigger place between here and Cripple Creek and my father was ranching. After he died, Mother had a hard time financially and every other way. Then Mr. Mallory showed up with money in hand, assuring her he was offering the best deal she could hope for, promising he'd take great care of the place. He even said he'd give her first right of refusal if he ever decided to sell it.''

''That doesn't sound so bad,'' Lark said, feeling duty-bound to give her father lip service, at least.

''It doesn't, does it? Unfortunately, Mom didn't get any of it in writing. It wasn't a good deal—he paid her a pittance, stole an inexperienced and grieving woman blind. Then when he got it, he didn't take care of the place. If Jared hadn't spent all his spare time on maintenance, the cabin would look like one of those tumble-down mining claims you find all over these mountains.''

''But Jared was paid for his work,'' Lark argued. ''It's not as if—''

''He was paid more for his silence than for his work,'' Jenny said bluntly. ''What he did to help the old homeplace survive was for love. Considering the time he put in, it probably worked out to something like a nickel an hour. But at least he was around to salvage the things your father kept tossing out—including furniture made by Great-grandpa Wolf, and all kinds of other mementos. Basically, your father just let everything go to rack and ruin. If Jared hadn't swallowed his pride, this would all be in ruins.''

''W-what do you mean, about Jared being paid for his silence?''

''Sorry, that I *can't* go into because it's not my place. But the very worst thing was, when your father decided to sell, he didn't say a word to us, just threw it on the market. Of course, he was mad at Jared at the time, but still, he went back on his word. When he found out Jared had bought the place through an intermediary, we heard he threw a fit, but it was too late. His excuse for doing what he did was that his deal had been with Mother and when she died, that cleared him of further obligation.''

For a few minutes the two women sat quietly, each lost in her own thoughts. Then Lark said a soft, ''I'm sorry.''

''You don' have to apologize for your father,'' Jenny said bluntly. ''You didn't do anything wrong. And actually... there's more. A lot more...''

Lark, unconsciously waiting for the other shoe to drop, held her breath and waited.

''Just before Mother died, she made Jared promise that he wouldn't go after your father for revenge. I think if she hadn't, Jared would have been on the first plane to Florida. But to Jared, a promise is a promise. From that day to this, your father hasn't stepped foot in the State of Colorado, that Jared knows of, anyway. If he had... if he does...''

She broke off with a shudder. ''Not to worry. All's well that ends well,'' she said cheerily. ''Don't you think we should stroll down there and see what those two have found that's so interesting?''

Lark didn't. All she wanted to do was sit here and ply Jenny with question after question about her brother. But instead she rose with a smile and together they walked down the steps and across the small meadow.

''Milk!'' Little Jared cried, his round cheeks turning red. ''I'm *furs*-ty, Mama.''

''Calm down for a minute,'' Jenny commanded. ''I'm trying to get this sticker out of Uncle Jared's hand.''

"On-too Jurd, I'm *furs*-ty!" The little boy turned his appeal on his uncle. Tears welled in his big, amber-brown eyes.

Jared kept his smile under wraps. "Sorry, sport, Mama's operating on Uncle Jared's poor little ol' hand. She may even have to amputate."

"Jerk." Jenny nudged him with her elbow but kept her attention glued to the fleshy part of his palm. "If you'll just hold still—"

Lark smiled uncertainly. "May I?" she inquired, glancing at the child. "I'd be happy to get this young gentleman a glass of milk."

"OK with me if it is with him," Jenny said. "Just don't get insulted if he won't go with you. It takes him a while to warm up to strangers and—"

She stopped short, for Lark had offered a hand and Little Jared grasped it in his own chubby one, then looked up with perfect trust. Lark cast a faint smile at brother and sister and led the boy toward the house.

"Will you look at that," Jenny demanded. "Kid'll make a liar out of you every single time."

"She does have a way with her," Jared admitted. He couldn't resist adding, "Better warn Little Jared not to let his guard down."

"Sorehead."

He felt the light scrape of her nails on his palm, and then she drew back with a triumphant, "A-ha! Got it."

He flexed his fingers and rubbed the spot where the thorn had been lodged. "Will I live, doctor?"

"Sure, as long as you treat Lark right." She cocked her head, her gaze level. "I like her, Jared."

"Good for you." He plopped down on the soft grass, knees bent, arms braced behind.

Jenny sat beside him. "She's not responsible for what her father did."

"Stay out of things you don't understand, Jen." He kept his voice flat and his features unruffled.

None of which fazed his sister in the least. "I understand more than you think I do. She's basically a very nice person, but she's vulnerable. I don't want her to get hurt."

"You think I might hurt her? Just how do you mean that?"

"I *mean*, she's a babe in the woods with a big bad wolf like you—" She looked startled, then burst out laughing. "You *are* the big bad Wolf in these parts, nobody would deny that. But this time I want you to have a heart. In fact, I insist on it."

"That's what I like about you, baby sister. You're always good for a laugh."

Jenny looked serious. "She's an interesting person, Jared, a nice person."

"A dumb person. She got herself lost out there in the forest a while earlier today. If I hadn't been following her, there's no telling where she might have ended up."

"A natural enough mistake for a tenderfoot."

He grinned; he couldn't help it. "I showed her a track at a water hole and told her it was a wildcat."

"A wildcat!"

"Don't get excited. It wasn't a wildcat, it was a badger."

Jenny stared at him incredulously. "But a badger has a tiny little print like this—" she held a thumb and forefinger three or four inches apart "—and a wildcat's got feet like—" She spread her hands, exaggerating the difference.

"Could have been a little cat." He laughed out loud, remembering the way Lark had shrieked and grabbed his arm. "The point is, she hasn't got a clue. She's got about as much business here as—as you do on a Caribbean cruise."

Jenny's eyes narrowed and she jumped to her feet. "I belong any damned place I care to go, and so does she. Give her a break, okay?"

It was an order. She headed for the cabin, striding angrily away with her back rigid. He watched her go, unperturbed by her show of temper.

She'd raised some intriguing questions and didn't even know it. He, too, found Lark interesting, but more for what he sensed than what he saw.

Years ago, he'd judged her the best of the bad lot of Mallorys. The old man was a son of a bitch, his wife—the first one, anyway—had been a secret drunk, Risa had been a flirt and a tease, but Lark . . . Lark had been a nice little kid. What had happened to her since?

It was as if all the fight had gone out of her somewhere along the line. Well, he thought, rising to follow his sister, everyone has limits.

What would it take to find Lark's?

CHAPTER FIVE

"ANOTHER cup of coffee?" Lark held out the coffeepot, hoping to delay Jared's departure this morning. For the three days since Jenny's visit, he'd eaten breakfast and disappeared, returning only as dusk was falling. Even yesterday's thunderstorm hadn't driven him back early.

He'd also been cool to the point of rudeness. Lark was going out of her mind trying to think of a way to jolly him out of it. She was thinking about him so much, in fact, that she'd hardly thought at all about her father or her fiancé or the mess she'd left behind in Florida.

Jared hesitated, and she thought he was going to turn her down. Then he shrugged. "Sure. Why not?"

She poured his coffee, then refilled her own cup, savoring even this small success. Sitting across the breakfast table from him, she found herself unable to meet his steady gaze.

The silence lengthened, stretching her nerves along with it. Finally, when she could stand it no more, she blurted, "So what are you doing out there in the woods all day every day? You're not even coming back for lunch."

Which she faithfully prepared, only to be disappointed.

"I'm doing what I came up here to do," he said calmly.

"Which is?"

73

One corner of his mouth curved up. "Get back to my primitive self. Back to nature, if you prefer."

"Oh." She couldn't help feeling offended that he preferred nature's company to hers. Although she wasn't exactly going crazy with loneliness, she did miss him when he was gone and eagerly awaited his return.

He sipped his coffee. "I'll never starve out there, if that's what worries you. I could live off the land if I had to, but it's never come to that. When I'm here, I always spend considerable time in the wild. I've got supplies and equipment cached all over the place. I only spend nights here in the cabin to accommodate you."

"M-me?"

"Wouldn't you be frightened here alone?"

Maybe not if she'd been alone since the beginning. But she'd grown accustomed to having him around and she liked it. So she nodded. "I suppose I might. Looking back, I can see that my family vacations here might have been anywhere for all the advantage we took of it. The forest and mountains were simply something to admire from the deck out back, and the animals were little more than strange sounds in the night."

"Your parents kept you close," he agreed. "On the other hand, you could have got into serious trouble roaming out there. As it was, I didn't have too much trouble keeping an eye on you and your sister." He leaned back in his chair and crossed his arms. "I've got this theory that you can find out a lot about people by observing how they react in a wilderness setting. Some take to it as if they'd come home, some go to pieces. Others, like your father, think they can fight anything, even the laws of nature." His expression challenged her. "Where do you fit in, Lark Mallory?"

She shivered. "I don't know," she said with painful honesty. "I've never had a chance to find out. But I wouldn't put money on my potential as a mountaineer."

He looked exasperated. "Why do you keep putting yourself down that way? It gets real old, real fast."

"You should know better than anyone, after saving me the other day."

"But you went out into the woods by yourself, and when I found you, you didn't seem all that scared to me."

"That's before you pointed out the wildcat tracks— and the fact that I was on the wrong trail."

"Oh, yeah, the cat tracks." He looked as if he were about to say more on that subject, but changed his mind. Finishing off his coffee, he stood up. "There's another reason, too."

"Reason for what?" Don't go, she pleaded silently. Talk to me.

"Reason I'm gone all day."

"Oh," she said, disappointed. "And that is?"

"You said you've got some serious thinking to do. I want to let you get to it."

With a heavy heart, she watched him walk out of the cabin and trot easily up the slope toward the aspens. Serious thinking... yes, she had it to do. If she could just stop thinking about Jared Wolf long enough to get started.

Four days later, as they were finishing up a dinner of fried chicken and potato salad, Jared issued a startling invitation.

"Want to come stargazing with me tonight?"

He'd been typically silent during the meal and the sudden sound of his voice startled her so much she dropped her fork. "Stargazing?" she repeated in astonishment.

"Sure. Looking at the sky?" He pantomimed the action. "Peering at the cosmos?"

That made her laugh. "I don't remember the last time I peered at the cosmos," she conceded. "But where? How...?"

He poked his fork into a chunk of potato, looking almost embarrassed. "I've got a homemade telescope set up at Lookout Point," he explained. "Growing up in these mountains gave me an appreciation for the wonders of the universe." He glanced up suddenly, pinning her with his gaze. "If you don't wonder, you're dead." He shrugged, as if he didn't care what her response might be, one way or the other. "Of course, if you're reluctant to wander through the woods in the dark of night with a virtual stranger—"

"I want to go," she interrupted quickly. "I was just surprised you asked me." Surprised and delighted. "And you're no stranger, Jared. I've known you since childhood."

Saying the words, although they might be technically true, brought a sudden acknowledgment that she didn't really know him at all. She'd had no idea he was interested in astronomy; she didn't know what kind of education he had, didn't even know for sure what he did for a living, although she assumed he'd followed in his father's footsteps as a small-time rancher and sometime mountain man.

"Where do you live when you're not here?" she asked impulsively. "Obviously you don't stay in the cabin year 'round."

"I invited you stargazing. I didn't invite you to intrude upon my privacy." He pushed his plate away and stood up, his whole manner indifferent. "I'll be leaving in thirty minutes. If you want to go, wear your boots and bring your jacket. It gets chilly out there even in August."

He turned and walked out of the kitchen.

She was not only ready, she was eager. With the path dimly lit by the steady beam of his flashlight, she followed him up the slope and into the trees. At first the night seemed abnormally quiet but as they passed deeper into the wilderness, she began to sense, and then hear, the myriad sounds of the forest.

She stumbled over a root and threw out one hand to catch herself against his broad back. He stopped, waiting for her to regain her balance. When she had, he grasped her hand and slapped it against his narrow waist.

"Grab a belt loop and hang on," he ordered. "We've got a bit of rough ground up ahead."

She did, quickly establishing a rhythm that made the going easier. Her movements seemed to mesh with his; with her knuckles pressed against his lean waist, she seemed to sense his movements before he even made them.

They entered a meadow and he switched off the flashlight. In the suddenly complete darkness, she plowed into his back, automatically sliding her arms around his waist while her cheek pressed between his shoulder blades.

For a moment he stood stock-still. Then he drew her around beside him. "There's plenty of light from here but we'll need to give ourselves a chance to adjust," he said in a low, cool tone. "Our eyes don't work like an automatic camera, adjusting instantaneously. The pupils have to dilate for at least ten minutes before we get our best night vision. All you have to do is relax, Lark. Relax and let yourself see...."

She took a deep breath, closed her eyes for a few seconds and opened them again. She didn't think this was going to work but if he told her to try, she would try.

To her astonishment, she discovered that he was right. Silvery moonlight and the glow of a million stars flowed around her, over her, and into her, sharpening her sight and her senses. All the objects in the night sky seemed to hang so low that she was tempted to reach up and grab a handful of stars.

"It's...glorious," she breathed, head thrown back, arms flung wide. "Oh, Jared, thank you for bringing me here!"

His laughter rang with satisfaction. "I'm glad you feel it," he said, "but you ain't seen nothin' yet. Take my hand and I'll lead you to Lookout Point."

She looked down at the hand, open and waiting for hers. Without hesitation, she slipped her hand into his, their fingers intertwining.

Yes, she thought, this is right. Whatever else in my life may be wrong, this is right.

And she followed him across the moon-and-star-drenched meadow and into the unknown.

* * *

"Do you see it? Over there to your right—Ursa Major."

Lark peered into the telescope, concentrating as hard as she could. "All I see is the Big Dipper," she confessed, disappointed because she knew he would be.

She felt his laughter through his hands on her shoulders. "Sweetheart, Ursa Major *is* the Big Dipper. You're doing great. Just relax and stop trying so hard, OK?"

His use of the endearment sent a warm glow spiraling through her. She felt almost drunk, dizzy with a combination of celestial beauty and his approval...not to mention his touch, impersonal though it might be.

She'd lost all track of time but they'd been at Lookout Point long enough for him to bring the telescope, which he'd set up earlier in the day, on-line. A ten-incher, he'd explained, with an altazimuth mounting which allowed him to move the telescope tube up and down and around.

As if any of that made the least sense to her. Yet, she listened with utter fascination, drawn along by the man and his enthusiasm.

He leaned closer, his chest teasing her shoulder blades lightly. "Move a little this way," he said, his arms coming around to guide her. "You should be able to see—"

"Ursa Minor," she chimed in, adding with a self-deprecating chuckle, "I catch on quick."

"Ursa Minor, the Little Dipper," he agreed. "Okay, let's see if we can find Cassiopeia...."

And Andromeda and Pisces and lots of other constellations. Concentrating fiercely, Lark peered through the telescope until her muscles were so tight she had to straighten to relax and stretch them.

"Wow, that's hard work," she said, rubbing her neck.

She felt his hands settle on her shoulders, his fingers digging into the tightness there.

"You're making it hard," he murmured, his hands working some kind of magic that relaxed one kind of tension while increasing another. "I've got a blanket here in my pack. Why don't you kick back over there on that big boulder? You can try some old-fashioned stargazing while I check out the scope."

It sounded good to her. She let him spread the blanket—not a blanket, actually; a sleeping bag, but she didn't blame him for not saying so—and settle her onto it before returning to the telescope. With a sigh, she lay back on the gentle lower slope of an enormous boulder and stared up into the heavens.

"It's . . . it's breath-taking," she murmured in awe. A bright light flashed past and she gasped, "Look! A shooting star!"

"Actually a small meteor, but who's counting?" He sounded amused. "You can catch a couple of 'em an hour around here, on any given night."

Just when she thought he'd dismissed the subject of shooting stars, he added, "Did you make a wish?"

"I didn't have time," she said ruefully. "I'll think of one now and file it away. Then the next time I see a shooting star—falling meteor, I mean—I'll have an all-purpose wish handy."

"Worth a try."

He didn't ask what her wish would be, for which she was grateful. She didn't know herself. To solve her Florida dilemma? To stay in Colorado forever? To stay beyond reach of her father forever?

To get lost in Jared Wolf's arms and never come out?

For a while they remained silent, Jared working with the telescope and Lark so deeply engrossed in the celestial panorama above her head that she began to feel as if she were floating up there among the stars.

After a while, she said, "Are you sure you're not really an astronomer disguised as a free-lance mountain man?"

His warm chuckle reassured her that he wasn't offended. "Why would I want to be a professional stargazer when it's the amateurs who have all the fun? The pros spend so much time with mathematics and physics that they don't have time to look up."

"So you just do this for . . . for fun?"

"This has been my idea of a good time since I was just a kid. I think I was about nine, ten, when I set up my first telescope here. I've been coming back ever since."

"Even during the years we—my family and I were in your cabin?"

"Of course."

"I never knew."

"Why should you? You were in your own little worlds, all of you. Besides, astronomy is sort of like my . . . my guilty pleasure. Looking up clears my brain, helps me solve problems. I thought it might help you, too."

"H-help me?"

Suddenly she no longer felt lazy and at ease; less so, when he turned toward her. Leaving the telescope, he walked to the edge of the boulder upon which she lay and leapt lightly up to sit beside her. In the clear, night light, he looked cautious and guarded.

He leaned over her, blotting out the sky, blotting out everything except himself. "Thoreau said something about how we need 'the tonic of wilderness.' It's true, at least for me."

"H-Henry David Thoreau?" she ventured, clenching her hands into fists at her sides to combat the desire to reach up and slide her arms around his neck.

"The same. There's nothing on earth as wild as what's up there." He reached out to stroke the line of her cheek. "The last frontier, as they say." His hand curved around her jaw, fingers insinuating themselves beneath her hair. "Well, maybe not the *very* last frontier."

He lowered his head slowly, giving her every opportunity to pull away, but moving with an assurance that told her any such move on her part would have been a surprise to him. To her, too. She'd been waiting for this kiss ever since the last-first time. Now she found herself rising to meet him, her lips eager for the touch of his.

Without a sound, he took her into his arms and kissed her with a hungry passion that sent waves of heat coursing through her veins. Clinging to him, she gave herself up to pure sensation, letting him lead, eager to follow.

At last he lifted his head and she heard his harsh breathing. Half opening her eyes, she saw him as a shadow in the foreground of a sky dripping with diamonds in a fantasy world.

"Please..." she murmured, then stopped; she had no idea what she was asking. That he stop? Ridiculous! That he continue? Impossible!

"Answer me this," he said into the silent night. "Are you still engaged?"

Her heart stopped beating and she lay there in his arms, struck dumb. Of course she was, in actual fact, until she informed those who waited half a continent away for her to come to her senses. But in her heart, she realized the decision had been made.

She could never marry another man, feeling as she did about this one.

But what to say to him now? "I—" she began hesitantly.

"Don't bother to come up with a plausible lie." He dropped her back onto the sleeping bag, slid over to the edge of the rock and dropped off, landing lightly on his feet. "I told you, I don't make moves on other men's women, even when they're coming on to me."

"Coming on to you!" She sat up, indignant that he would suggest such a thing. "I never—"

"You didn't want me to kiss you just now?"

She scooted down the rock, pulling the sleeping bag with her. The night, formerly so brilliant and full of comfort, seemed to grow cooler and more forbidding by the second. "I—why, I never thought—"

"The hell you didn't."

Reaching up, he caught her around the waist and lifted her the rest of the way. Holding her against his body, he slowly lowered her to her feet, making sure she felt every ridge and surface of his taut body. Even when she stood breathless before him, he didn't let her go, instead wrapping an arm around her waist.

He said one word with a contempt that cut her to the core. "Liar."

This time his kiss was rough and hard and quick; again, any protest she might have made was lost in a flash of feeling. Pulling back, he spun away from her.

"I rest my case," he said in a bitter voice. "You're a Mallory, sure as hell."

She struggled to keep up with him on the dark trek back to the cabin. Miserably unhappy, unable to concentrate on where she was going, she stumbled again and again. Her plight obviously aroused no sympathy from him, for he plunged ahead, pausing with ill-concealed impatience only when necessary to keep her headed in the right direction.

By the time they reached the cabin, she was exhausted, not to mention scratched and battered by limbs and weeds and bushes and brambles which had torn at her hair, her arms, her legs. Once inside, he neither looked at her nor offered to light the lamp, simply headed up the stairs to his bedroom.

That night for the only time she could remember, Lark cried herself to sleep. Even when her parents had separated, even when her mother died, she hadn't collapsed the way she did now.

What a fool she was, she berated herself, lying alone in a darkness far less comforting that what she'd found at Lookout Point. Why hadn't she faced the inevitable? Even before she left Florida, she'd known in her heart of hearts that she didn't love Wes and shouldn't marry him—couldn't marry him, after meeting Jared Wolf. Not to please her father, not to provide herself with an easy and comfortable life, not for all the gold in Fort Knox could she marry Wes Sherborn.

She thought of Jared and her heart began to race. When had her case of puppy-love turned into the real thing? She didn't know; all she knew was that if she'd been strong when she should have, she could have given Jared the answer he'd demanded of her at Lookout Point. She didn't expect he'd give her another chance.

Regardless of that, she knew what she had to do. Tomorrow she'd tell him she was breaking her engagement, and then she'd do it. Whether that would change Jared's low opinion of her, she had no idea. In a larger sense, it didn't matter, for even if he threw her out of here on her ear, she still couldn't marry Wes Sherborn.

She couldn't marry anyone except Jared Wolf, and he was never going to ask her. A man from what he described as "a long line of happy marriages" had little patience with a woman he thought would take an engagement lightly.

But maybe...just maybe, she could change his mind about that.

She had no chance to find out, for when she awoke the following morning, he was already gone. She knew a moment of panic; now she wouldn't even be able to coax him into driving her to the Mountain Mom 'n' Pop Store so she could make a telephone call.

Then she discovered his car keys lying on the hand-carved oak table in the front room. For a moment she stood there clutching the key ring, wondering if she dared take his Land Rover without his permission. She wouldn't want to make him angry—

And then her chin rose with new determination. She had to do it; she had to call Wes and tell him it was all over between them. Even if she never saw Jared again—her heart constricted at the thought—she had to do the right thing.

So she'd take his vehicle and hope for the best. And she'd do it now, before she could change her mind.

Driving down the pass, her anxiety increased with every passing minute. By the time she pulled into the dirt parking lot before the little log store, she trembled so badly she had to sit there for a few moments before she could pull herself together enough to climb out.

The telephone in its old-fashioned booth stood just inside the door, a concession to the weather, she supposed. With her stomach in knots, she pulled her telephone card from her wallet and punched in a multitude of numbers. Three rings, and a crisp voice droned, "Mallory and Sherborn Development Corporation. How may I help you?"

"May—" Lark swallowed hard and started over. "May I speak to Wes Sherborn, please?"

Was the hesitation just a shade too long? "One moment, please," the operator said in the same impersonal voice.

So it was all right, Lark thought with relief. Wes would answer; Wes would understand.

And she wasn't simply telling herself this to ease her conscience. He *would* understand, she was sure of it. It was her father who would never—

"Lark, where are you? Dammit, you've worried us all to death, little girl."

Oh, God! Her call had been routed straight to her father's office. She grabbed the small shelf beneath the wall-hung telephone to keep from sagging to her knees.

"Father?" Her voice came out an incredulous croak. She couldn't believe she was actually speaking to him. "I asked for Wes."

"I'll tell Wes anything he needs to know. So when will you be home? I've had my hands full, keeping this quiet. You've got a lot of explaining to do."

Lark closed her eyes against that old, sick feeling. More than anything in her life, she'd wanted this man's approval. She'd never had it, and now she never would. But despite that, she would do what was right for her, and for Wes, too.

So she said, "I'm not coming home. That's what I called to tell Wes. The wedding is off."

"The hell it is!" She could imagine her father in full fury, his face suffused with angry color. "Are you in Albuquerque? You get your fanny back here so we can get this straightened out. I'm not going to stand by and let you throw away your future—"

She hung up on him. For a moment longer, she leaned against the telephone, feeling weak as a kitten. She'd rarely defied her father and never successfully.

Maybe this time, things would be different.

Jared hadn't returned. He still hadn't returned, and she had so much to tell him.

Pacing through the cabin, she searched for something to do, anything to occupy her hands and her mind, but everything was in apple-pie order. For the dozenth time, she walked out onto the deck in back and scanned the trees; nothing. Where he was or what he might be doing, she couldn't imagine.

All she knew for sure was that if she didn't find something to occupy herself, she'd go crazy. What she needed was a massage, or a nice long soak in a hot tub, or—

The hot springs! She'd go to the hot springs and immerse herself up to her nose in swirling mineral waters.

She hesitated, her hand on the railing. Could she find it? Last time she'd tried, she'd blithely struck the wrong trail. If it hadn't been for Jared, no telling what trouble she might have been in.

But this time is different, she assured herself. He'd pointed out her mistake, and now she knew where she'd gone wrong. She glanced at her wristwatch. It was only two p.m. She had plenty of time. She'd move carefully, pay attention to landmarks. She'd find Wolf Springs, enjoy a nice long soak and be back, a new woman, before Jared even returned.

If he ever did return.

No, don't think that, she warned herself, hurrying down the outside steps and across the meadow toward the trees. She didn't even bother to return for a towel, so eager was she for action, any action. Her muscles screamed for action, as did her mind. She was, quite simply, a mass of nerves.

One thing she knew for sure; the status quo was killing her. She had to do something, even if she did it wrong.

How could she have gotten confused the other time? This time, the trail seemed as obvious as a freeway. Through the aspen she went, on into the firs, circling around the densely packed lodgepole pines and plunging into a stand of spruce and scrub oak.

And suddenly there it was: water spilling over one moss-covered rock after another to reach the lowest level. Tree-shaded and serene, Wolf Springs looked exactly as she remembered it—perhaps the only thing that did.

Peeling off her clothes, she sat down on a boulder and poked a toe into the deeply blue waters roiling below—hot, yes, but not too hot. A sense of tranquillity stole over her. With a sigh of grateful surrender, she slid into water up to her chin and closed her eyes.

Here, surely, all her cares would be washed away and she would emerge a new woman with new thoughts and new directions.

High above the sparkling pool, partially hidden by a cluster of boulders near the top of the ridge where the springs began, Jared Wolf watched Lark Mallory through narrowed eyes. Then he began to move carefully down the slope. . . .

CHAPTER SIX

THE soft scuff of a footfall on rock brought Lark swinging around in the water in surprise and panic. A tall, forbidding figure loomed above her, silhouetted against the sky like some forest lord. Sunblind, heart in her throat and arms crossed protectively across her breasts, she stared with horrified fascination.

"*What in the hell do you think you're doing?*"

She slumped with relief. It was Jared, of course, not some mountain marauder come to carry her away. Even the angry edge to his inquiry failed to alarm her, although she did sink lower into the luxurious warmth of the water. "What does it look like?" she countered defensively.

"It looks," he said in that same dangerous tone, "like an invitation."

She caught her breath on a little gasp of understanding. "Maybe... maybe it is," she whispered before she could stop herself.

Her eyes had adjusted and she could see him clearly now, see him reach for the buttons of his plaid shirt. Holding her breath, she watched him strip off the garment and toss it aside.

Was this what she'd been waiting for all along? She turned away, her heart thundering beneath her protective hands. The strength of her feelings for Jared Wolf both frightened and excited her—but she must call it by its true name, now.

Love. She loved this man. Although she had no reason to hope he would ever return that love, she was prepared to risk everything to belong to him at least for a little while.

She felt his presence in the small pool. His entry agitated the water, sending little waves lapping around her throat. And then his hands settled over the slick wet skin of her shoulders, pulling her against him. With a groan, she let her head fall back while her legs tangled with his.

He leaned closer into the curve of her shoulder, his lips and breath tickling her ear. "I thought I was strong enough to withstand any temptation but I ... was wrong. There's nothing in this world that can stop me from making love to you right here and right now—nothing, not pride nor principle, not even admitting that my passion for you has overcome my scruples. Only you can stop me. Do it now, Lark Mallory. Say the word or be prepared to take the consequences."

For a moment she trembled beneath his light hold. Then she drew a shaky breath and turned to face him, the gossamer veil of shimmering, steaming water all that separated them. Unable to resist, she curved her hands over his strong jaw, cupping his face.

"I won't say the word because this is right," she whispered. Rising on tiptoe, she peered into his eyes, willing him to believe her. "You were my first love, Jared. I think I've belonged to you all my life, at least in my heart. Now I want to belong to you in fact."

She let the swaying water carry her closer, until her body brushed his with light insistence. "I've missed you," she murmured. "There's so much I want to say to you, including the fact that I lov—"

"No more talk." He brushed a wet finger across her lips in erotic reproof. "Actions speak louder than words."

And indeed they did....

Lark sat on a boulder which jutted out over Wolf Springs, fully dressed at last and none too happy about it. Jared stood on the ground beside her, wearing his shoes and jeans but no shirt. His torso, at eye level, was magnificent; smooth and bronze and a mass of washboard ripples.

She felt a secret little smile curve her lips. She knew that torso now, that body, that man. Knew him and loved him. Whatever the future held, she would never allow herself a moment's regret for what had passed between them here at this magical place.

He tilted her face up for his kiss. "No regrets?"

"None. Jared, I tried to say something before, something important, but you didn't let me finish. I'd like to say it now—"

"I don't want to hear it, Lark."

Stunned, she stared at him. "But—"

"I know what you're going to say." He was looking past her, into the trees.

"But...but you couldn't. It happened while you were gone. I realized then that I—"

"That's enough!" He thrust one hand through his damp hair, shoving it back. "Don't try to sanctify what just happened with meaningless words. Saying you love me, that your engagement was a mistake, that your rebellion against your father has nothing to do with what we shared, isn't going to make it true."

"But you don't understand." Rising to her knees, she threw her arms around his neck. "This has nothing to do with my father. It's you I—"

"I'm not interested in your lies, Lark. What just happened was pure physical gratification between consenting adults, nothing more. Great sex—no strings attached. If you insist on rationalizing and sugar-coating it, I'm out of here."

His words were arrows aimed directly at her heart, but she dared not protest. He'd do exactly what he said; if she insisted on revealing her true feelings, he'd turn around and walk away into the wilderness for who knew how long. And if somehow she managed to blurt everything out, he wouldn't believe her anyway.

In a flashing instant, she knew she had no choice. More than she wanted to unburden herself about her call to her father, the broken engagement, her love for the man in her arms, she wanted even more to keep him near. And so she forced herself to sink back to her knees on the rock, although she couldn't stifle the sigh that escaped her lips.

"You win," she said in a ragged voice.

"I expected to." He slid one hand around her back, beneath her damp hair. "Don't look so unhappy, sweetheart. We both know the score. Why do you women always have to tie everything up in pink ribbons?"

"Maybe the same reason you men are afraid to deal with your feelings," she murmured, rubbing her cheek against his wrist.

"Depends on which feelings." He wrapped an arm around her waist. "I don't think I'll ever come to this place again without getting . . . feelings."

"Is this the first time you ever . . . ?" She fumbled for a way to say it. "You know, ever . . ."

"Made love here?" His chocolate-brown eyes laughed at her. "Yes. Although I doubt we're the first couple to take advantage of the obvious."

"Really? Who else, do you suppose?"

"You want names? I'd guess my parents, my grandparents, my great-grandparents, to name a few. I think one of the reasons my great-grandfather chose that particular site for his cabin was the nearness of the hot springs." He shrugged. "But you're not interested in Wolf family lore."

"I am so. I think it's fascinating." *I think anything and everything that has to do with you is fascinating,* she thought, knowing he wouldn't want to hear that. "Please go on." She could listen to the mellow sound of his voice forever.

Jared looked into the depths of the pool as if at something only he could see. "Wolf Springs is special for many reasons. The Utes believed spirits lived deep in the earth. The hot springs were sacred because that's how the spirits showed themselves. Every year, tribes would gather at the hot springs for all kinds of rituals." He added matter-of-factly, "Of course, that was before they were pushed out by white settlers."

"That's terrible," Lark said indignantly, "not to mention unfair."

He glanced at her, then burst out laughing. "Some white men really *did* speak with forked tongue," he drawled, "but not all. Same goes for white women. But my great-grandpa and my great-grandma found each other in spite of everything, remember? They settled on this land and beat the odds by living happily ever after. Proves it can be done."

He jumped off the rock, then turned to lift her down beside him. "It's starting to get dark. We've stayed way longer than I intended."

She looked at him through the curtain of her lashes, deliberately provocative. "What *did* you intend when you crept up on me that way?"

"Little witch," he said, smiling. "I intended to give you hell and send you back to the cabin in tears, never again to venture forth alone."

She slid her arms around his waist. "Got a little more than you bargained for, didn't you?" She hardly recognized that husky voice, or the forwardness of the woman who kissed his throat with lingering attention.

"Yeah," he admitted. "I did. You know..." He sucked in a ragged breath. "I don't suppose we have to get back to the cabin *this instant.*"

He scooped her up in his arms and carried her with long, determined strides to a velvety patch of grass. There she was destined to receive yet another lesson in what it meant to love this man.

They strolled back to the cabin through the dusk, hand in hand. They didn't talk; there seemed little left to say at this point.

Resolutely, Lark pushed her only problem from her mind; not her father, not Wes, but Jared, and his refusal to listen to her explanations or declarations.

Well, she thought resolutely, she would play the game his way because she must. But when the time was right, she'd tell him that he hadn't betrayed his own principles by making love to another man's woman. It did, however, give her bittersweet pleasure to know that even thinking the worst, he'd succumbed to his desire for her.

Perhaps he'd learn to care for her as well as want her, she thought wistfully. But she dared not count on that. Better to take what he was willing to give, and not pin her hopes on more, than to have her heart shattered completely when it was over.

She shivered.

"Cold?" He slipped an arm around her shoulders and led her down the final slope to the cabin.

Leaning against his warmth, safe in the shelter of his arm, she knew that nothing could be better than this . . . except possessing his love.

That night he moved her into his bedroom—and his bed. "Goldilocks," he teased, holding out his arms. "Come to Papa Bear."

"You mean, Papa Wolf," she retorted.

But she went, and happily, although she had to bite back the words she longed to say each time he held her close: *I love you*.

Over breakfast on the morning of their third day as lovers, Jared announced his intention to go into Cripple Creek. "We need a few supplies, more than I can get at the Mom 'n' Pop Store, and I've got a couple of phone calls to make," he said. "Thought you might have business to take care of, too."

"Oh!" Lark had pushed all thoughts of Florida and that other life right out of her mind, but she immediately realized he was right. She'd only spoken to her father, counting on him to announce her decision to cancel the wedding and the engagement; she had no idea what he'd told Risa or Wes. "I should call home."

"They got a clue where you are?" he asked too casually.

"They think they do. Father took the bait—he thinks I'm in Albuquerque, which suits me just fine."

For a moment he just looked at her. Then he said, "You'll have to face it sooner or later, Lark. There's rarely good to be gained by putting off something unpleasant."

She had no answer to that.

They set out at midmorning, through a glorious August mountain day. Reaching Cripple Creek, Jared drove straight to the Miner's Repose Hotel, instead of turning up the hill to Jenny's little house.

"She's working today," he explained in answer to Lark's inquiry. "Just want to let her know we're here, and see if she can join us for lunch."

The hotel was glorious, all restored Victoriana with royal blue carpeting and flocked wallpaper in the lobby. Jenny presided behind an elaborately carved and curved registration desk—and what a Jenny!

With her long black hair piled atop her head, her shapely figure enhanced by a white shirtwaist and long black skirt, she might have stepped from the pages of a 19th-century ladies' fashion book. When she saw her brother and Lark, she hurried around the desk to greet them with open arms.

"This is a wonderful surprise," she exclaimed.

Lark smiled. "Jenny, you look fabulous. Are you sure you weren't born in the wrong century?"

"No—in fact, I'm sure I *was*. I've been told I greatly resemble my great-grandmother, Molly, and I feel more comfortable in these clothes than my own."

She lifted her long skirt and extended a foot, shod in a dainty high-button shoe. "Only problem is, they make me wear shoes here."

"Mighty unreasonable for a girl who'd rather run around in her bare feet," Jared agreed. "Jenny, think you can join us for lunch later? That's why we stopped by."

Jenny was staring at the two of them and didn't seem to hear. Jared repeated his invitation with no small irritation in his tone.

"Oh, sure, sure," Jenny agreed. "I can get away in an hour or so. You two—" She looked from one to the other with a frown. "Something's changed."

What Jenny might think she saw, Lark couldn't imagine. She and Jared weren't touching, hadn't said a personal word to each other since they'd entered, hadn't even exchanged a tender or knowing glance. Still, such an astute comment flustered her.

Jenny's eyes suddenly went wide. "You're... together!" she exclaimed. "That's what's different."

"Don't be an idiot," Jared snapped, his impatience barely concealed. "We've been together for— how the hell long's it been? Weeks?"

Jenny was shaking her head vigorously before he even finished his defense. "No, big brother, I mean *together*." She gave Lark an impulsive hug. "But this is wonderful!"

Feeling like an impostor, Lark accepted the hug. Jenny was right in sensing a new intimacy, but wrong if she thought that indicated an equal degree of commitment. "It's not what you think," she began.

"Dammit, Jen," Jared cut in. "You're making a spectacle out of the lot of us."

"Don't be an old fogy." Jenny did, however, glance over her shoulder. "Look, I have to get back to work or Mr. Grover will have a fit. Meet me here at one, okay?"

"Sure." Jared took Lark's arm; then, at Jenny's knowing glance, dropped it like a hot potato. "Mind if we go pick up Little Jared? He's at Miss Willie's, right?"

Jenny nodded. "Good idea. He'll like that. See you later." Blowing a kiss in their general direction, she returned to business.

Lark followed Jared out of the Miner's Repose, half glad and half sad Jenny had guessed their secret so easily. On the one hand, Lark was proud to be chosen by a man like Jared Wolf; on the other, she was sorry he'd chosen her to share his bed and not his life. But of course, his sister couldn't know that.

Little Jared was just finishing his lunch—peanut butter sandwich, a glass of milk and a bowl of applesauce—when Jared and Lark arrived to spirit him away. His elderly baby sitter, Miss Wilhemina Porter, aka "Miss Willie," greeted them with pleasure.

"He's been a good boy and deserves an outing," she said, washing his smudged little face before releasing him from high-chair captivity. "He had a late nap this morning so he should be good for a couple hours."

"On-too Jurd!" The little boy held out his arms for his uncle's embrace.

To Lark's surprise, Jared hauled a child's car seat from the deepest recesses of the Land Rover and proceeded to buckle the chortling youngster securely in place. Heading down the hill toward town, she asked a question that had been on her mind since first meeting Jenny and her son.

"I don't mean to pry, but I can't help wondering about Little Jared's father."

"I figured you'd get around to asking about that." Jared turned onto Bennett Avenue.

"Please don't think I mean any criticism," she said hastily. "Jenny's a wonderful mother and Little Jared's a doll." He also made her weak with baby-hunger every time she held his firm little body in her arms, but she wouldn't say that. "I just can't help wondering."

Jared steered the vehicle into a parking space along the curb in front of a casino. "You and me both," he muttered. "I don't have any more idea who the kid's father is than you do. All I know is, Jenny came to me one day going on three years ago and announced she was going to have a baby—and she was damned well going to keep it. Shocked the hell out of me. Not that boys hadn't been flocking around Jenny since she was just a kid. But she never gave any of them a tumble, that I could see."

"How... brave."

"Brave, hell. Jenny's a Wolf. We do what has to be done, brave be damned."

What was that supposed to mean? "Really, Jared, you might give her a little more credit. It was *very* brave of her to face that kind of responsibility alone—"

"Horsey!" In the backseat, Little Jared jumped up and down in his car seat, pointing furiously. "Horsey!"

Sure enough, an open carriage pulled by two gray horses was passing them and pulling to the curb just ahead. Two couples, obviously tourists, climbed down.

"Horsey!" Little Jared shrieked, his face turning red. "I wanna ride the horsey!"

Lark smiled at Jared. "Yes, *horsey!*" she echoed the child's plea. "Please, Jared, Little Jared and I want to go for a carriage ride!"

Jared looked disgusted. "Well, hell," he muttered. "I can't fight both of you."

Hand in hand, Little Jared and Lark followed Jared to the carriage. The driver, a young man with a bushy beard and friendly blue eyes, smiled down at the threesome.

"Howdy, Jared. How's it goin'?"

"Not bad. This hack for hire?"

"Hell," the driver said wryly, "it's free but tips are gratefully accepted."

"There'll be a big one in it for you if you take my nephew and my—" Jared cast a guarded glance at Lark "...friend for a nice, long ride."

"You got it, man." The driver straightened. "Climb in and let's get this show on the road."

Jared helped Lark and Little Jared into the white-painted and canopied carriage. Lark settled onto the plush red upholstery and hoisted Little Jared onto her lap, holding the wiggly child firmly around the waist.

Jared climbed in and lowered himself gingerly beside her. The driver clucked to his team and the carriage pulled away from the curb. There was almost no vehicular traffic, although many cars were parked at the curbs and pedestrians milled around on all sides.

Little Jared was so excited that he bounced up and down on Lark's knee. And in truth, she was excited, too.

"I've never ridden in a horse-drawn carriage before," she confessed, giving Jared a shy glance. "This is fun."

He shook his head. "You amaze me."

"Me? Why?"

"I wish I knew." He leaned back against the cushiony upholstery, frowning.

But she thought she saw a hint of satisfaction beneath his surface disapproval. For whom was Mr. Jared Wolf putting on an act, her or himself?

The carriage meandered up Bennett Avenue, past casinos with names like "Wild Bill's" and "The Brass Ass" and "Bronco Billy's." Wedged into the row of gambling parlors were other businesses: antiques, souvenirs, T-shirt shops and so forth.

Even the people they passed looked different, not a part of the twentieth century at all. Many of them were in costume, and Lark surmised these were employees of the various establishments. Others were either tourists, like the kids in their cowboy outfits with six-shooters strapped to their waists, or locals like the grizzled prospector-type ambling across in front of the carriage.

The old-timer stopped in the middle of the street, only an arm's length from the passing carriage. "Howdy, Wolf," he said, touching the stained brim of his hat.

"Slim." Jared returned the greeting and the level stare.

Seeing the two men size each other up, Lark almost laughed. They seemed so right for this time and place, but they'd have looked equally at home here a century ago. Indeed, that old-time boom town was booming again, this time mining tourists instead of gold.

"How did Cripple Creek get its name?" she asked suddenly, sure Jared would know.

He didn't disappoint her. "That's kind of a long story, starting with a little old creek at the edge of town. That creek got its name when a cow tried to jump it and broke a leg. When gold was discovered nearabouts in 1890, Cripple Creek Gold Mining District was formed."

"Then the town sprang up and—voilà!"

"Not exactly." He grinned, his arm on the back of the carriage seat slipping lower, until it was around her shoulders. "The town was originally named Hayden Placer, but they did eventually wise up and change it to Cripple Creek."

"That's wonderful!" Lark didn't even try to temper her admiration. "Is there anything about these mountains you don't know, Jared Wolf?"

The coach driver snickered and his beefy shoulders shook with muffled laughter. "Hardly nothin'," he called back. "Ask him about Pearl Devere, why don't you?"

"What about Pearl Devere?" Lark repeated innocently, although judging from the driver's leering tone, she thought she could probably guess.

Jared glanced warningly at the toddler on her knee, then at her, his dark eyes sparking with mischief. "Pearl Devere was a well-known...sportin' lady who opened a—" he cleared his throat "—*parlor house* in Cripple Creek not long after the discovery of gold in the 1890s. She called her house on Myers Avenue the Old Homestead, and she was the...uh...boss."

"A parlor house?" Lark raised her brows.

The driver guffawed. Jared shrugged.

"Oh, the Old Homestead was one of the finest," he said airily. "It was undoubtedly the most popular...resort...in town."

The driver spoke over his shoulder. "That Pearl must'a been a pistol," he said in admiring tones.

Jared nodded. "She was probably into charity work," he agreed. "When she died, the town gave her a rootin', tootin' funeral, complete with a mounted police escort, a twenty-piece Elks Club band, and practically every miner in the district in attendance. Her girls—I mean, her employees were heartbroken, so the story goes."

Lark gave him a serene smile. "It's always good to hear of a woman succeeding in business," she said sweetly, hugging Little Jared.

The flash of approval on Big Jared's face warmed her to her toes.

"I can hardly believe you let Lark lure you into doing the tourist thing," Jenny remarked with a smug smile.

Jared glanced after Lark, wending her way between dining tables to reach the telephone in the hall, before glowering at his sister. "It was Little Jared's idea," he said brusquely.

"Little Jared gets the same idea every time he sees a horse," Jenny agreed calmly. "This is the first time you've given in. But if you want to deny what's plain as the nose on your face—"

Jared tossed his fork onto the red tablecloth. "I don't give a damn what—"

"Jared, watch your language!"

Both glanced at the child, busy crumbling saltine crackers over the edge of the high-chair tray and not paying them the slightest heed. Since he'd already had his lunch, he wasn't hungry but he was having a good time playing with the tidbits they'd offered.

Jenny patted her brother's hand. "I'm sorry. I'm not trying to make you mad. Hey, I'm delighted! It's been a long time since you had someone special in your life."

"Special? Don't jump to conclusions."

"I don't think I am." She sighed, a long, drawn-out sound. "I really envy you, big brother."

"What the hell—heck—for?"

"The way she looks at you sends shivers down my back. The poor misguided soul thinks you walk on water. Lucky she doesn't know you like I do."

Her attempt at levity failed miserably. Jared resisted a desire to reach out and shake some sense into her. "You haven't got a clue what's going on here," he snarled. "I'll give you a piece of advice, baby sister—don't get too attached to her because she's a Mallory and she's not going to be around that much longer."

"What's that supposed to mean?" Jenny's blue eyes grew wide. "Jared, you're not planning to use her to get revenge against her father! Because if you are—"

Before they could get into what he was or was not planning, Lark, face pale, reappeared in the doorway and conversation stopped cold.

The telephone call to Risa had been far from satisfactory. As usual, it had begun with, "Where are you?" and ended with, "You can't run away forever!"

In between, Lark discovered that her father hadn't calmed down, hadn't canceled the church, and hadn't even told Risa or Wes about the most recent call, the one Lark thought had settled everything.

"My God," she'd said to Risa, "Wes doesn't know? I've got to call him right away—"

"Save your nickel," Risa advised. "He's visiting friends in Key West. There's no way you could track him down today. I'm not even sure when he'll be back. Try him in a day or two."

"But I can't!"

"Why not?"

"Because there's no—" Several tourists chose that moment to stream past, chattering away at the top of their lungs. Lark hunched over the telephone, covering the mouthpiece until they'd disappeared into the dining room.

"Where *are* you?" Risa had repeated, this time suspiciously. "What's all that noise?"

"That's not important," Lark said. "I just want you to know I'm not coming back to Florida—ever."

Risa gave a little shriek of dismay. "Wes still thinks he's getting married August thirtieth. You've made an awful mess of this, Lark. A lot of people are going to get hurt."

You have no idea how many or how much, Lark thought. "I'm sorry," she managed to force past stiff lips. "You know I don't want that, but I can't go through with the wedding, not now." Maybe before she knew what love really was, but not now. Not after waking up in Jared Wolf's arms.

But then a new and horrible realization struck her; she'd let Jared make love to her under false pretenses after all. She'd thought her engagement was cleanly broken, that she'd severed those entangling ties that bound her to the wrong man. Instead, she'd been deceiving herself. Every doubt he had about her was justified.

She felt like a failure. But there was still a way out, albeit a cowardly way. "Risa, you've got to do something for me," she said abruptly.

"Oh, Lord, now what?"

"Tell Wes the wedding is off. Tell him I'll call as soon as I can to explain everything, but in the meantime, there's the church to cancel, all the food and flowers—"

"I can't do it. It's not my place. No, you've got to do it yourself."

"I can't! I will not be physically within reach of a telephone for the next several days, and this has to be done as soon as possible. Please, Risa, I have no one else to turn to. I'm begging...you've got to do this for me."

After a few tense moments, Risa groaned. "I suppose I can try."

"Soon? You can't imagine how important this is."

"I can't?" Risa was almost sputtering in outrage. "Remember, I'm the one who's here, watching everybody going nuts."

"Oh, God, I'm sorry. I didn't mean to imply you weren't suffering, too. But I...I have to hear you say it, Risa."

"All right! Stop pushing. Just remember, you can't keep running forever."

Lark knew that, but she'd also convinced herself that she was growing stronger with every hour's reprieve. Thanking her sister profusely, she ended the call and hurried back into the dining room. One look at the faces of her luncheon companions told her they'd been having words. Anxiously she pulled out her chair and sat down, looking from one to the other.

Jenny poked at her salad. "Everything all right in Florida?" she inquired, sounding cross.

"Butt out," Jared interjected. To Lark, he added, "You about ready to go?"

"No, she's not about ready to go!" Jenny flared. "I promised her a tour of the hotel."

Jared's dark eyes flashed. "We don't have time for that," he said impatiently.

"But you have time to go traipsing up and down the street in a horse-drawn carriage? Don't make me laugh! You're just bent out of shape because *someone* might see through you. What's so all-fired important that you have to get out of town in the next five minutes?"

"Please, both of you—"

Jared quelled Lark with a hard glance before swinging on his sister. "Jenny, you've got a bad habit of opening your mouth before your brain's engaged. You expect me to let you live your life, now let me live mine. When I want your opinion, baby sister, I'll ask for it."

"Why, you overbearing, sanctimonious, insensitive—"

Lark glanced at Little Jared, afraid he'd be frightened by the raised voices and challenging words. The child seemed oblivious to the altercation as he continued to bang his spoon on the tray, sending cracker crumbs flying in all directions.

Jared stood up, his face chiseled from stone. "That does it," he said from between tight lips. "We're getting out of here."

His angry gaze locked with his sister's for a moment, then swung toward Lark. "You coming or not?" He didn't look as if he gave a damn, either way.

Jenny looked equally determined to stand her ground. Neither would yield, neither would back down.

What am I doing, getting mixed up with people like these? Lark wondered. *I really don't know this man at all.*

But what little she knew, she loved; what she didn't know, she could barely wait to find out. Slowly she stood.

"I'm sorry, Jenny," she said. "I guess we'll have to do the tour some other day."

CHAPTER SEVEN

LARK slept alone in Jared's bed that night, for after a silent supper he'd just disappeared into the darkness. Tossing and turning hour after hour, she agonized over her situation.

Which was, quite simply, that of a woman in love with a man who could not seem to trust her. Not that she entirely blamed him. If only she'd broken her engagement before leaving Florida—as she now saw, very clearly, she should have done.

She arose the following morning without answers, more exhausted than when she'd retired. Strangely enough, she couldn't see that exhaustion in her face when she looked into the mirror. Frowning, she peered more closely.

And saw to her astonishment, that she'd never looked better in her life. She'd gained a few pounds since arriving in Colorado and that gaunt, haunted look was gone from her eyes, the hollow cheeks had filled out. But the biggest change was in the expression; the woman in the mirror looked back at her with a level, determined gaze.

That woman was surely stronger than the one who'd let herself be victimized by circumstance. What's the worst that can happen? Lark asked the face in the mirror. Even if she had no future with Jared, nothing could ever make her sorry to have known him... loved him.

Is it better to have loved and lost or never to have loved at all? At least she had the answer to that age-old question: to love! Smiling, she walked downstairs and into the kitchen—

Where she found Jared sitting at the table, calmly eating cereal out of his favorite mixing bowl. Where he'd spent the night, she had no idea. He looked up without a trace of emotion in his dark eyes.

"All right," he said, as if picking up a previous conversation at midpoint. "Tell me."

She clung to the back of a chair, once again thrown off balance. "T-tell you what?"

He shrugged. "Whatever you want, whatever it is you've been trying so hard to say. I've been putting you off but now—" Something flickered in his eyes. "I'm all yours."

She wished. Suddenly dry-mouthed, she sat down. "All right. Back there at the hot springs—"

"On that fateful day?" His brows rose.

She managed a nod and a weak smile. "I wanted to tell you that it was all right, that I'd broken the engagement."

His eyes narrowed and a new tension seemed to settle over him. "Oh, really?"

"What you said about other men's women— I wanted to tell you that there no longer *was* another man. I wanted t-to tell you—" This was turning into the hardest thing she'd ever tried to say. Dared she declare the depth of her feelings for him?

"When?"

"When, what?"

"When did you break the engagement?"

It was clear that he still hadn't decided whether to believe her or not, trust her or not. "Just before I went to Wolf Springs that day. I drove your Land Rover to the Mountain Mom 'n' Pop and called—''

Called Wes, but her father had intercepted her. Was it her fault he hadn't passed on the message?

"You talked to what's-his-name?"

"His name is Wes." Dared she lie? Dared she not lie?

"That's it, Wes. You talked to him?"

Well, no, but that wasn't her fault, it was her father's. Now Risa had promised to do the evil deed. Did sending two messengers equal one face-to-face encounter? *What should she tell Jared?*

"I'm waiting for an answer." He was, his face like stone, his arms crossed over his chest.

"Wes knows!" she blurted. "I feel bad enough about this. Can't you just let it go at that?"

"Did you say it flat-out, no room for mistakes, that you're not going to marry him? Because if you didn't and you want to go back and pick up where you left off, your secret is safe with me. Great sex, no strings, remember?"

She wanted to slap him for that; it took several moments to regain control of herself. Then she gave a stiff little nod of denial. "I don't want to go back."

He stood up. "Anything else?"

"Isn't that enough?" she countered, *I love you*s no longer seeming appropriate.

Did he believe her? She couldn't be sure.

Although she hadn't told him the literal truth, she'd been honest about her intent.

Wes would know by now. What difference did it make, whether she told him herself or he heard it from a member of her family? As long as he got the word that the wedding was definitely, completely, irretrievably canceled, she was telling Jared the truth...at least in spirit.

Did he believe her? No.

Did he want to believe her?

Standing on the rise behind the cabin a couple of days later, Jared thought about his increasing involvement with Lark Mallory. No strings, he reminded himself, *no strings*.

He'd slept out in the woods for the past two nights trying to decide about her. He'd meant what he said; he didn't chase other men's women.

And he didn't make love to liars, at least, not if he could help it.

Turning, he trotted into the aspen grove. It had rained earlier in the day and he was soon soaked by the moisture clinging to leaves and shrubbery, but he didn't slow his pace.

He needed to know the truth before this affair went any further, and he knew only one sure way to get at that truth.

It took just twenty minutes to reach the Mountain Mom 'n' Pop Store by foot, cutting through the woods. Once there, he sequestered himself in the small telephone booth just inside the front door and dialed information for Palm Beach, then the Sherborn-Mallory Company headquarters.

When the receptionist answered, he asked for Wesley Sherborn. After a brief pause, a smooth male voice came on the line. "This is Wes Sherborn. What can I do for you?"

"I'm trying to reach Ms. Lark Mallory. I understand you're a friend of hers."

"That's right. Who is this?"

Jared hesitated. This call had everything to do with Lark and nothing to do with her father. The time wasn't yet right to draw Mallory to Colorado.

Even so, Jared saw nothing to gain by lying about his identity. He didn't know Wes Sherborn and Wes Sherborn didn't know him—had never even heard of him. Lark doubtless had a lot of friends; what were the chances that this guy would mention this particular call to Drake Mallory?

The chances, Jared decided, were nil. So he said, "My name's Jared Wolf. You could say I'm an old friend."

"What do you want with her?"

"I hear she's getting married in a couple of weeks."

"That's right, August thirtieth. To me." The man chuckled as if well pleased with himself.

"Congratulations."

"Thanks. So what was it you—?"

"Thought I'd send her a wedding gift...for old times' sake."

"I'm sure that will please her. Just send it to our new place—wedding present from her father. The address is—"

Jared stood perfectly still. He'd wanted to know for sure.

Now he did.

When Jared didn't come back, Lark panicked. Throwing caution to the wind, she lifted his car keys from the mantel and drove the Land Rover into Cripple Creek.

She was crazy, she told herself as she drove along. Crazy, first of all, to take a chance on finding Jenny at home. If she was at work, or shopping, or even off somewhere playing with Little Jared, Lark would be risking Jared's wrath for nothing.

No, not for nothing. If she didn't talk to someone about the mess she'd gotten herself into, she'd go out of her mind. Maybe she'd get lucky.

And she did. As she parked the Land Rover in front of the little house on the hill, Jenny came outside onto the porch in her bare feet, smiling and waving a welcome.

Gratefully Lark followed Jared's sister inside and accepted a tall glass of lemonade. With Little Jared napping, the two women carried their glasses out onto the porch. They settled there in the shade, the magnificence of the Rocky Mountains spread out before them.

Jenny spoke after a while. "What's the matter, Lark? You look miserable."

"That's because I am." Lark bit her lip.

"Jared's driving you crazy," Jenny suggested wisely.

"How'd you guess?"

"It's plain as the nose on your face that you're head over heels in love with him."

"Plain to everyone but him. Oh, Jenny, sometimes I wonder—" She broke off.

"Wonder what? Lark, you can talk to me. I promise I'll keep your confidence. I don't know if I can help but I'm willing to try."

"That's sweet of you, but there's nothing you can do. Jared simply doesn't trust me. I don't know if it's just me or his hatred for my father, but something's always between us. No strings, he keeps saying—no strings. Well, I want strings!" She almost choked on her own unhappiness. "I don't like being treated like a one-night stand. I'll take it if it's all I can get, but I don't like it!"

Jenny looked aghast. "Surely that's not how he treats you."

Lark nodded decisively. "It is. He doesn't respect me because I'm engaged—was engaged when I got here—" She stopped in confusion.

"*Was* engaged or *are* engaged?"

"God, at this point I don't even know." Lark slumped in her chair. "I've tried to tell Wes—that's his name—twice and ended up sending messages both times, once by Father and the other time by Risa. I can only hope Wes got them. Because in my heart, it's definitely *was*."

"I can see how much this is hurting you."

Lark sighed and closed her eyes. "I'm not the only one, unfortunately. Wes and I should never have gotten engaged to begin with. But we've known each other forever, and he proposed in front of my entire family, and his, too. There just didn't seem any way to get out of it gracefully. And my father was so pleased...." She felt the prickle of tears behind her eyelids. "I've tried all my life to get that kind of approval from Father, but marrying the wrong man just to make him happy—well, I can't do it. I thought I could but I can't."

"Are you close to your father?"

"Close?" Lark thought about it. "No. I want—wanted to be..."

It all came spilling out, then, feelings she'd never put into words before. "My parents separated when I was fourteen—right after we returned to Florida from our last family vacation at Wolf Cabin, in fact.

Father wanted Risa and me to stay with him and I wanted that, too. Mother... Mother was drinking too much and that scared me."

"But you went with her anyway. Why?"

Lark didn't like remembering how hard it had been to make that choice. "She needed me and he didn't," she said at last. "He had Risa, who was always his favorite, so I moved to Miami with Mother. Father was furious, of course. He said things about her, awful things, while he was trying to get me to choose him." She shivered. "I think he was mostly guessing, but he turned out to be right."

Once started, the words poured out. "From the minute Mother and I moved away, Father was after me to spy on her for him. The pressure was awful but I managed to keep my integrity... until almost the very end."

Jenny leaned over to pat Lark's hand with gentle encouragement, but said nothing. Her expression said it all.

"A couple of years after the breakup, Mother smashed her car into a tree. She'd been drinking, which wasn't unusual. She'd stopped trying to hide how much, at least to me. I was in the hospital waiting room. No one would tell me anything—I didn't know if she'd live or die. Father was called, of course, and he started right in on me. I should have chosen him, look what she'd done to herself, she could have killed me, too. She wasn't worth my worry, I'd never made a decent decision in my life and should have trusted him, that kind of thing.

"I started screaming, actually attacked him—I think I really wanted to scratch his eyes out. I shouted that I didn't blame Mother for the things she'd done, with him always in the background making her life a living hell. And I told him, chapter and verse, that Mother *did* drink too much, and she *did* have men coming and going—"

Lark looked up at the blue, blue sky with all its fluffy white clouds and her voice dropped to a lower, calmer pitch as if to mitigate the worst part. "I betrayed her, and at that very moment, the doctor walked in and said she was dead. I lost it completely."

A sheen of tears made Jenny's blue eyes shine. "But you were just a kid. Listen, Lark, you can't blame yourself for any of that."

"I was sixteen, and I did blame myself. Maybe if I'd told Father what was going on, he could have helped her. Maybe if I'd told him . . ." She shook her head to clear away those racking doubts, knowing *now* that there had been no right or perfect thing she might have done, yet feeling the guilt and pain all over again.

"Father took me home with him and Risa. Instead of yelling at me like I expected, he sat me down and explained chapter and verse why I should never again trust my own judgment. He said I was weak, just like my poor, deluded mother, who drank too much and fell for every good-looking man who came along. He said I was lucky to have a father with my best interests at heart, and that not all fathers would take back such an ungrateful child.

"He said that he knew it wasn't my fault, that my mother had turned me against him. And I didn't correct him, God help me. I let him think that horrible lie was the truth.

"Risa understood what I was going through. She advised me to let him believe whatever he wanted, try to get along with him and just get on with my life.

At the time, I thought it was good advice and I tried to take it. Now... I'm not so sure."

She turned to Jenny, saw the melting sympathy on her face but dared not let that breech the dam holding back a million tears. "I stopped fighting then. After a while, I think I forgot how. It was easier to give in than it was to take an unpopular stand and the emotional battering that went with it. God, Jenny, when you and Jared go at it, my hair practically stands on end."

"Honey, that's how our family's always operated. Everybody says their piece and walks their own path. But just let anyone else take after one of us, you'll see a united front! We're all very outspoken and we say exactly what we mean, but we love each other and we don't hold grudges."

"That's... inconceivable to me."

"Then it's no wonder you and Jared are having a hard time of it."

"He isn't, I am. He seems to know exactly what he wants and precisely how to go about getting it. He makes the rules and I play by them except...."

"Except?"

Lark met Jenny's steady gaze. "You know Jared and I... we're lovers. Or at least, we were."

Jenny smiled. "No need to sound defensive about it. I'm not judging you—I couldn't." She glanced toward the house where her fatherless son lay sleeping. "I was in love once myself. The choices I made then weren't always the ones my family would have had me make. But they stood by me and I don't regret it, because I have a child I love more dearly than—than life itself."

"No regrets..." Lark sighed. "I have so many regrets, but none about loving your brother. When I first got here, I saw no reason to tell him I was engaged—I mean, there was nothing between us. By the time I realized my mistake, it was too late. I've never seen a guy with so much respect for the institution of marriage—even a promise of marriage. Not that it isn't wonderful, because it is. But it's sure hard to live up to."

"That's why he's still single," Jenny declared. "He told me once that he didn't want to settle for less than our parents and grandparents and great-grandparents had. I remember his exact words, because I was so irritated at him for demanding perfection when he wasn't so blasted perfect himself—he's not!" she added when Lark started to rise to his defense. "I love my brother, too, but he's no angel!"

Lark laughed ruefully. "An angel, no. That I'll concede."

"Thank you," Jenny said primly. "What he said was, 'you just can't trust women to sign on for a lifetime anymore.' He said," and she launched into an impersonation of her brother, "'I don't want to make any mistakes. I'll be damned if I'll settle for one of these disposable marriages you see today.'" In her own voice she added, "What a shame. If there was ever a man meant for family life, it's my brother."

They sat for a few minutes in silence. Then Lark said, "Thank you for listening, and not passing judgment on me."

"Honey, you've already passed judgment on yourself, and it's a harder one than you'll ever get from anyone else."

Lark shrugged. "I don't know about that, but I think—I know Jared doesn't respect me because I don't have the guts to stand up to my father. Jared doesn't run from anyone or anything, which is one of the qualities I admire so much about him. But I'm not like that. It was cowardly, but when I ran away from Florida it was the only way I knew to get the space I needed to sort everything out."

"And have you?"

"Oh, yes!" Lark clasped her hands in her lap. "Knowing Jared, falling in love with him, has given me the strength I needed to stand up to my father—" She added with a rueful laugh, "At least long distance. I've burned my bridges. I couldn't turn back now, even if I wanted to. Which I don't."

But even as she said those brave words, Lark wasn't quite sure they were true. As long as Jared was beside her, she could face anything. But Jared hadn't made up his mind. What if he turned against her?

What then?

For two more long, horrible days, Jared stayed away from the cabin. Lark thought she'd go out of her mind, waiting for him, watching for him. When he did walk through the door, she didn't wait for him to indicate his state of mind, didn't wait for a signal, just threw herself into his arms and clung to him.

"I was so worried," she cried. "Thank heaven you're here."

"Has something happened?"

With her cheek pressed against his chest, she couldn't see his face. But she felt his alert response to any suggestion of danger.

"N-no," she admitted, "nothing except I missed you and I'm so glad you're back."

For a moment he simply held her in an embrace so tight it felt as if he'd never let her go. Then he said, "So that's the way you want to play it."

"I'm sorry?" She leaned away enough to see his expression, which was as blank and unreadable as a new chalkboard.

"Don't look so worried. I'm back."

"Y-you don't seem very happy about it."

"Happy?" He set her away from him, out of his arms. "No, I'm not happy. As the lady said, I've still got a lot of thinking to do."

Jared seemed as wary as always but Lark sensed something else in him, something she couldn't quite define. She thought about him while she made the tuna salad sandwiches for lunch the next day.

It was as if he'd made a conscious decision to take things as they came, cross one bridge at a time. In the meantime, he'd been watching her with new caution...and after that first hug, which she'd initiated, he hadn't touched her again.

It wasn't all she wanted but she could live with it, if she must.

She had no warning of his approach until he walked through the back doorway, in off the deck. She glanced at him and a greeting froze in her throat.

He looked at her for a moment, his expression full of speculation. Then he said bluntly, "What would you do if your father found you?"

The plate of sandwiches fell from her numb fingers to crash and shatter on the floor. She felt frozen, immobilized by his question, which somehow seemed more like a prediction.

He looked at her with dark, expressionless eyes. "So what would you do?" he prompted.

What would she do? Now, when she was just beginning to hope again? "I couldn't face him," she choked. "I'm not ready!"

Jared's dark brows soared. "That's a bit dramatic, don't you think?"

"You don't know. You just don't know how he intimidates me." She gripped her hands against the rising panic. "I'm afraid I'd end up letting him bully me into something I don't want unless—" Her wide, hopeful gaze sought him out in supplication. "Help me, Jared. You could stand up to him. I think you could stand up to anybody."

He took a step back, shaking his head. "I have no reason to fight your battles for you."

His words inflicted new wounds on her heavy heart and her head sagged. "No, I don't suppose so."

"So you'd just give up, let him haul you back to Florida like a naughty child." He sounded cynical and only mildly interested.

"What else could I do?" She flung back her head and cried in a trembling voice, "God, do you really think he'll find me? I thought I was in the clear. How—?"

"There are a million ways he could track you down," he said, dismissing further speculation along that line. His eyes narrowed. "You're just delaying the inevitable, you know that. Running away is never an answer."

"In this case, it's the only answer." She looked helplessly at the mess on the floor, realizing she should clean it up but incapable of knowing where to begin. "I know it's hard for someone like you...someone so sure of himself...to realize how I feel. With a little more time..."

But she was kidding herself, not Jared. She was no closer to getting out from under her father's thumb than she'd been when she arrived.

"Why not bite the bullet and stand up to him?" Jared bared white teeth in a grimace. "You can act like an adult, for once, and tell him to get the hell out of your life."

"You're making this sound like a certainty." She gazed through the window at the path leading into the woods, and a new thought began to form. "The forest has been a second home to you since you were a kid," she said slowly. "You have food, all kinds of things stashed out there."

"No." He emphasized the word with a shake of his head. "I don't run from anybody."

"We could—we could camp out. It'd be fun."

"Stop it, Lark. You don't know what you're saying."

"But—"

"Probably he won't show up. Forget I mentioned it."

"Forget?" She laughed incredulously. "I have a horrible, sinking feeling that tells me I don't dare."

He simply looked at her, his eyes veiled. "One of these days, you're going to have to do something if you do it wrong."

She licked dry lips. "When I know my own mind better...then I'll do something."

* * *

And when I'm ready, I'll do something, Jared thought—if it's not too late. Standing on the ridge behind the cabin, he examined the road below for any movement. Ever since his telephone call to Florida, the feeling that he'd made a mistake had grown from a distant possibility to a certainty.

His enemy was close; he felt it. Although his lust for revenge remained unabated, he was not yet sure what form that revenge should take.

Or how much hurt he was willing to inflict on Lark to bring her father to his knees.

Alone and unstrung, exhausted by sleepless nights full of endless worry, Lark climbed the stairs with weary steps. Lying with her head on his pillow, breathing in the familiar masculine scent of him, she stared at the ceiling.

After a while, she slept.

When she awakened some time later, it was to the sound of angry voices.

CHAPTER EIGHT

JARED Wolf stood on the front porch of the cabin, staring down at his arch enemy through slitted eyes. Drake Mallory was a big man with florid coloring that had become even more pronounced over the years. He looked a little older, a little heavier, but not significantly different.

He was still the same arrogant, powerful man he'd always been.

"Well, well, well," Mallory said with angry malice. "If it's not the errand boy. Where the hell is she, Wolf?"

Jared controlled his own temper with an effort. "Who you talkin' about, Mallory? You meeting another one of your women here?" He rubbed a flat hand against his thigh, his gaze locked with that of the other man. "Nah, that can't be it. Both your wives found out about your little trysts and divorced your—"

"Keep my family out of this!"

"Glad to, if you'll just get the hell off my property."

The two men literally strained toward each other, although Mallory didn't put a foot on the bottom step and Jared didn't put a foot on the top one. Their long history of antipathy tested the bounds of civility almost to the breaking point.

Mallory gestured angrily toward the house, from which he was effectively barred. "I know my daughter's in there and I'm not leaving until I speak to her. You've got no damned right—''

"I've got every right in the world, up to and including property rights. She doesn't want to talk to you."

"You always were a lying—"

"Watch it. I'm not a kid anymore, and you're no longer king of this mountain. You've got nothing to hold over my head, you arrogant, obnoxious—'' Jared bit down hard on his anger. "You'll have to go over me to get to her and I don't think you're man enough to do that." A very slight smile curved his lips and he added softly, "Although I'd sure as hell like to see you try."

Mallory took an involuntary step back. "Dugan!" he shouted over his shoulder. "Get over here!"

Jared started; he'd been so intent upon Mallory that he hadn't even realized another man was in the car. Now he saw that it was Slim Dugan, one of the wiliest old mountain men in the state.

And one of the smartest, too. Slim climbed out to lean against a fender of the shiny new Jeep. A grin creased his weathered face. "No, sir, thanks a lot, Mr. Mallory," he drawled. "B'lieve I'll stay right where I am." He added with a nod, "Howdy, Wolf. You're lookin' tolerable."

Mallory bared his teeth in a growl of frustration and swung back to face Jared. "If you've hurt her, so help me, I'll see you dead."

"That's no way to talk when you're trying to make a deal." Jared's scornful laugh tore at his throat. It was all he could do not to hurl himself down the steps at his enemy's throat. "Why would I hurt her when her family was always so good to mine?" he asked gently. "Hell, just because her daddy lied and cheated and hassled my mother into her grave—" He stopped, breathing through his nose, his teeth clamped together. "Then there was *her* mother, blaming all the empty liquor bottles on me . . . and her sister, letting me take the blame when—!"

Whirling, he banged one fist against the peeled wood of the porch support. "Get out of here, Mallory," he grated. "Go. Go now!"

Mallory looked stunned by the force of Jared's animosity—stunned and, for the first time, worried. "Not until I know she's all right," he insisted doggedly. "For all I know, she's being held here against her will. I wouldn't put anything past you."

"Past the half-breed, you mean," Jared inserted bitterly.

"Dammit, I want to see my daughter! I want to hear from her own lips that she doesn't want to talk to her old dad. I know once she sees me, she'll be reasonable." The man crossed his bulky arms across his chest and planted his feet wide. He looked frightened and determined in equal parts.

"No."

"At least ask her. If she'll just—" Mallory thrashed around for an approach that stood a chance of succeeding. "Hell, if she'll just come to the window and throw a rock at me—I don't care. But until I see her, I'm not budging. And if you don't give me some satisfaction, I'll be back—with the law!"

Jared hesitated. He'd be perfectly content to let the bastard make good his threat but he didn't think Lark would really want that. She had to be awake by now; she was probably hovering behind the open second-story window.

Dammit, she *should* talk to her father! If somebody would just stand up to him once in a while, it'd do him a world of good—not to mention the good it'd do those he'd been browbeating for years.

"All right," Jared decided suddenly. "I'm going to give Lark the pleasure of spitting in your eye herself. But if she says no—" His level, challenging stare made it clear; no one was going to force her to do anything she didn't want to do. "Wait here."

Without another word, he turned and disappeared into the interior of the cabin.

She was gone.

He didn't know when, he didn't know where, but she was gone. For a moment he stood at the back window through which she'd obviously exited by climbing down onto the deck before taking off in God only knew which direction.

It really wasn't that difficult a decision for him to make.

She'd packed quickly, grabbing socks, a sweatshirt, a windbreaker, her extra pair of jeans, T-shirts, underwear. Stuffing everything in the backpack she'd found discarded in a corner, she tossed her driver's license and a few toiletries on top, then crept to the front window.

"*That's no way to talk when you're trying to make a deal,*" she heard Jared say.

He was selling her out; she didn't have much time. She had no recourse but to sneak out the back window. She could find her way to the Mom 'n' Pop Store, she was sure of it. Once there she could phone for—what? Who? She'd worry about that when the time came!

She had never felt such a sense of urgency, not even when she'd left that bridal shop in Palm Beach and found herself standing in line at an airline ticket counter. Then she hadn't known where she was going or what she would do when she got there.

And here she was, still running. Premeditated cowardice, she supposed miserably. She'd have to deal with that sooner or later, exactly as Jared had warned her.

Her choice was *later*.

Soon her breath came in short pants but still she ran, her backpack flapping against her and snagging on tree limbs. Stopping to catch her breath, she leaned gasping against a boulder and that's when she heard it: the sound of running feet. Someone was coming after her. In a blind panic, she bolted into the trees again.

He was upon her before she'd taken a dozen strides, grabbing her by the backpack and whipping her around in a circle. She tried to struggle free of the straps but he had her—

"Jared!" She nearly collapsed with relief, then remembered what she'd heard. Fighting to get away from him, she used hands and feet alike.

"Dammit, cut that out!" He finally subdued her with one strong arm securely around her waist. "I'm trying to help you!"

"You call that help? What kind of deal did my father offer you to bring me back?" She aimed another quick kick at his shin but missed.

"What the hell are you talking about? I didn't make any deals. He said he wouldn't leave until he spoke to you—said he'd be back with the cops and both of us know he's not above it. And in all honesty—" He looked pained. "I really couldn't blame him for wanting to be sure you're all right. He said he didn't care if you threw something at him through the window, so long as he actually saw you."

"Oh." Deflated, she sagged against his side. "But I thought—"

"If you'd hang around and ask questions instead of running off half-cocked all the time, you wouldn't get yourself into these messes."

Some of the icy chill was leaving her body. "You mean you weren't going to drag me downstairs and shove me in his car?"

He made a sound of disbelief. "You've got to be kidding. So, are you ready to go back now?"

"No! I don't want to see him. Jared—"

"Now what?"

"Let's stay here."

"Here, where?"

"Here in the forest," she said impatiently. "What better place to think—you said so yourself."

He released her and sat down on a fallen tree trunk. "Look," he said as if the words were wrung from him, "there's another option. I can get you back to civilization, to an airport or whatever. You can find someplace else to hide and start playing your little games all over again."

Civilization? What did she care for civilization? She had nowhere to go, nowhere to hide. Perhaps if there had been no Jared, she'd have learned to live on her own by now. Perhaps she'd even be ready to go back to Florida and take up the familiar strands of her life.

She didn't think so but anything was possible, as Jared was so fond of saying.

For better or worse, Jared was a part of her now, and would remain so as long as he would allow it.

"Please," she said humbly, kneeling before him. "I want to stay here with you. Tell me what I can do to make you believe me. Anything—just tell me."

He opened his arms. "You can kiss me," he said roughly. "Kiss me as if you mean it. That's the only way you'll ever convince me that I haven't entirely lost my mind to get between you and that arrogant swine you call your father."

Suddenly this didn't feel like "running away"; it felt like an adventure, a wonderful, once-in-a-lifetime adventure. Her spirits soared. This is going to be wonderful, she told herself as she followed him through brilliant mountain sunshine. This is not running away from something, this is running *to* something: a grand, never-to-be forgotten experience.

Her father had done her a favor by forcing them out of the cabin. She'd become too comfortable there, too entrenched. Compared to Florida, the cabin was primitive shelter; compared to the wilderness, the cabin was civilization personified.

She was too anxious and stepped on Jared's heels. "Sorry," she apologized breathlessly.

He gave her a dubious glance, then stepped aside and guided her past him on the trail. "Go on up to the edge of those trees and wait for me there," he ordered, turning to his right and stepping off the path. "Stay out of sight. I won't be long."

"Where are *you* going?" she asked in sudden panic.

"Back to the cabin to pick up a few things. I left in a bit of a hurry."

"But—won't he follow you?"

"I wish he would." The dark eyes narrowed, as if he were thinking of all the things he could do to a city man out here, without even half trying. "Slim Dugan's the one I'll have to worry about."

"That man we saw in Cripple Creek?"

"That's right." He gave her a pat on the fanny. "Go on, I can't do what I need to do until I've stashed you out of harm's way. Just stay put and you'll be fine."

She wasn't too crazy about being "stashed" like so much camping gear but he was the boss.

Now, more than ever before, he was the boss. So she found a spot inside the trees, behind a brambly bush that offered additional cover. Hunkering down, she eased her backpack to the ground and tried to catch her breath.

She was accustomed to the altitude now, and no longer huffed and puffed when she took more than a dozen steps. Her current breathlessness, she knew, was more the result of excitement than physical activity. As her breathing returned to normal, she began to relax and listen to the sounds of the forest around her.

The raucous cry of a bird was followed by a flash of blue feathers. A butterfly wafted past, its orange and black markings drawing her attention. Lark watched its erratic path until she lost it in the undergrowth, wondering how a creature so delicate and defenseless could survive in this world of predators.

Jared could tell her, if he were here. He never seemed at a loss for answers when the subject was the flora and fauna of these mountains he loved so well. When Jared returned . . . beautiful thought.

Jared slipped from the cover of aspens and glided across the open ground to the cabin's east wall, using all the speed and stealth he'd cultivated since childhood. He'd chosen his time carefully; at dusk, he'd be just one more shifting shadow on the mountainside. He'd already raided the outbuildings for the items they'd need, and had stashed those at the top of the rise, beneath the trees.

Pressing against the log wall of the main cabin, he stood perfectly still until he could be sure he hadn't been detected. Then he edged carefully around to the back of the cabin, where he paused beneath the open kitchen window. At first the sounds inside were nothing more than an indistinct murmur, but as he focused, he could make out two voices and most of the words.

"—should have killed the S.O.B. when I had the chance. . . . sorry now I didn't."

Mallory. That despised voice knifed down Jared's back.

"Hoss, I know you're exaggeratin' but you don't impress me none. If that boy was past ten when you bumped heads with him, you can thank your lucky stars you didn't get *too* far outa line. . . . clean your plow."

Dugan. Mallory had hired the one man in these mountains whose skills might be a match for Jared Wolf's—hell, were almost certain to be, since Jared was saddled with a tenderfoot woman. Jared would have to use everything he knew if Mallory unleashed the old mountain man on the trail of his rebellious daughter.

Of course, there was always the chance they'd stay right here, snug in the cabin and counting on the rigors of outdoor life to drive Miss Palm Beach back into her daddy's arms. But she'd changed in the time she'd been here, Jared thought suddenly. She was still running, but now he thought it might be more from force of habit.

"I can't believe she didn't even leave me a note."

Mallory, whining again. Old bastard thought the world revolved around him.

"Nah," Slim agreed, "but she sure as hell sent you a message. She don't want to see her daddy, that's plain as day."

"To you, maybe. How do we know that lousy half-breed didn't use force to get her to go with him? She probably wasn't even in the house when we arrived— hell, she probably doesn't even know I'm in Colorado. My Lark's sensitive, not the kind of girl to go running off into the wilderness on her own."

Slim's voice sounded steely. "And Jared Wolf's not the kind'a man who has to force a woman to do just about any damn thing that appeals to him. Look, he's no kin of mine and I don't have no personal stake in this, but I got a gut instinct tellin' me you're full of it... *Mister* Mallory."

"I'm not paying for gut instincts, Dugan," Mallory snapped, "I'm paying for know-how. Tomorrow I want you to go get my daughter and bring her to me."

"And if she don't want to come?"

"She will. I'll give you a note for her. All you have to do is make sure she reads it."

"...consider...a while to run that boy to ground."

"Whatever it takes."

The scrape of a chair leg indicated movement, and the conversation became harder for Jared to follow.

"...come back right enough. Of course, if...bring her anyway—own good. ...fine man waiting in Florida."

"...a damn whether...your note. Been a hard year...price is right."

The sound of footsteps crossing the wooden floor made Jared draw back a bit farther from the window. It was almost full dark now, but when you were dealing with Slim Dugan, it didn't pay to take foolish chances.

"Think I'll go out and have me a quick look-see." The voice was very near now, coming from just above Jared's head. "Be back in a couple'a—"

Jared was no longer listening. Streaking back across the clearing, he was already pondering what Dugan's entry into the game might mean.

And feeling the competitive juices start to flow.

"But I'm tired. I don't *want* to change campsites tonight."

"Really? Maybe you want to spend the night back at the cabin trying to explain to your daddy what the hell you're doing traipsing through the woods with a man who is *not* your fiancé?"

Lark blinked in confusion. "I told you, I'm not engaged to Wes anymore."

"That's right, you did mention that." Jared's tone dripped scorn. "Somehow I seem to keep forgetting."

She'd rise above his sarcasm. "What's going on down there? Isn't he going to leave?"

"We're not talking 'he,' it's 'they.' Don't forget Slim Dugan."

"So?" Sitting in the tangle of a sleeping bag, she pushed her hair out of her eyes and yawned. She hadn't realized how tired she was until she'd lain down "for just a few minutes" to wait for him.

She'd promptly fallen sound asleep.

He spoke with exaggerated patience. "The man your father brought with him is probably the best tracker I've ever seen, excluding an Indian or two."

"Tracker? You mean, my father's brought someone along to track me down like—like an animal? Why would he do such a thing?" Shocked and indignant, she sat up.

"He thinks I've kidnapped you."

Her mouth fell open. She snapped it shut again. "You're kidding!"

"Do I look like I'm kidding?"

"No." She peered at him through the moonlight. "From what little I can see, you look like you're *enjoying* yourself."

Silence. Then a low chuckle. "Maybe I am," he admitted without the slightest shame.

"*Why?*"

"Because," he said, kneeling to gather up their gear, "this guy is good. Under normal circumstances, I wouldn't mind seeing what he can do."

"I don't believe this." Lark leaned over to press her forehead against her bent knees. "I'm running for my life and you want to see if you're better than this—this rival mountain man?"

"I said, *under normal circumstances*, which these aren't. I'm looking forward to teaching your daddy that he can't have everything he wants when he wants

it—not anymore. Now haul your fanny off that
sleeping bag and let's get out of here while we still
can. There'll be plenty of time to argue when we get
where we're going.''

Only there wasn't. They traveled through the forest
for what seemed to Lark like hours, only to fall into
sleeping bags and rise at first light to set out yet again
for parts unknown. Her shoulders ached from the
backpack, her stomach growled from lack of a hot
meal, the blisters on her feet multiplied at an alarming
rate, but still they pressed on.

''Your choice,'' he goaded when they stopped at
midmorning for a drink from a crystal-clear mountain
stream. ''Old Slim is hot on our trail, but if you can't
take the pace, say so. Anytime you want to go crawling
back to Daddy, just say the word.''

She wouldn't—couldn't. They pressed on.

The place where they finally stopped running was one
of the most beautiful Lark had ever seen. Standing
in that high meadow, she clapped her hands in delight
and awe at the pristine beauty spread out before her.
Against a backdrop of evergreens, deer grazed among
clouds of purple flowers, while rugged mountain tops
loomed over the picture-postcard setting.

Jared knelt beside a cold mountain stream tumbling past in its rocky bed. Cupping one hand, he
scooped up water and drank. ''You did good,'' he
said without looking at her.

''I did?'' Lark blinked in surprise and gratification. A warm glow of pleasure spread through her
at even that faint praise.

''I wouldn't say it if it wasn't true.'' Standing, he
turned to a fallen tree extending across the small

stream and patted the trunk. "Come sit down over here and let me take a look at your feet."

"My feet?"

"You were limping when we got here. You've got blisters."

She hung back, for some reason embarrassed to submit her feet to his appraisal. "I'm all right," she fibbed, although her feet, especially her heels, felt raw inside her canvas and leather hiking boots.

He snapped his fingers and pointed to the horizontal tree trunk. "Sit. Feet are too important to take chances with 'em. You should have told me yours were bothering you. Hell, I should have noticed."

Still talking, he seated her and knelt to unlace her boots, drawing them off with surprising gentleness. "After I get you fixed up, we'll set up camp here. I'm fairly confident we're all right for the moment. Damn, I should have checked your socks."

"What's the matter with them?" She tried to peer past his hands to view the offending foot coverings.

He slid the socks off and stuffed them in his pocket. "No wonder you got blisters, wearing these flimsy little things. You need wool. Fortunately, I've got some extras. They'll be too big but I think I can adjust them so they'll still be better than those things."

Holding one of her slender, high-arched feet in a gentle hand, he used the other to pull the bandanna from around his neck. Dipping it into the icy stream, he bathed first one foot and then the other, paying particular attention to her heels.

Lark held her breath, first from the shock of cold water but then from the intimacy of what he was doing. No one had ever performed such a service for her. His touch kindled a glow in the soles of her feet that traveled up and up until her cheeks glowed with the same heat.

From his backpack he withdrew a small first-aid kit containing an ointment which he carefully spread over several tender places on her feet. He followed that with the application of adhesive bandages, then carefully smoothed wool socks onto her feet, his hands lingering on her ankles as he made adjustments.

At last he replaced her boots, laced them up and lifted her off the log and onto her feet. She stared at him with lips parted, never dreaming that a blister could lead to such a sensuous experience.

"Time to set up camp," he said brusquely, turning away.

He'd only been doing what was necessary to keep her healthy enough to maintain his pace. Anything else had been only in her imagination.

She could hardly believe how quickly he organized an efficient camp. Sitting cross-legged beside a small fire, watching him tie a fishhook to a line, she couldn't help saying so.

He looked up. "It is some advantage to lead a primitive life if only to learn what are the necessaries," he said.

She regarded him with suspicion. "Who said that?"

"Caught me." He smiled. "Thoreau."

"Your favorite."

"Yes. He also said that 'Most of the luxuries and many of the so-called comforts are not only dispensable but positive hindrances.'"

"I don't think I'd go quite that far," she said, tongue in cheek.

He shrugged. "To each his own—or her own, as the case may be." He finished tying the hook and put it aside.

"Are we safe now?" She finally asked the question most on her mind.

"'Safe' isn't the operative word. Your father wouldn't hurt you, and he couldn't hurt me. This isn't life and death, it's a game."

"To you, maybe." God, such confidence must be nice. "The man with him . . . If he's a friend of yours, why is he hunting us?"

"I never said we were friends." He tossed another small stick onto the fire. "Slim and I go way back, been on several rescue missions together. Couple of years ago we took off after a couple of lost hikers and the competition got a little out of hand."

She could just imagine. "Who got to them first?"

He threw back his head and laughed. "Somebody else! While Slim and I were messing around trying to throw each other off the trail, somebody else found them. It was no big deal—they weren't in danger or anything. But Slim and I took a lot of ribbing about it."

"I see." She nibbled on her lower lip. "I suppose he's being paid."

Jared nodded. "If Slim had lived a hundred-and-fifty years ago, he'd have been a true mountain man—but if he'd lived only a hundred years ago, he'd have been a gunfighter. Yeah, he hires out for all kinds of work. Thing about Slim is, he doesn't get emotionally involved. He just does his job and walks away."

"Does he have a family?"

"None that I know of. He lives way back in the hills, sometimes doesn't come down for months at a time. But when there's tracking or hunting or trapping to be done, Slim Dugan is your man. Everybody who spends any time around here knows that. On the one hand, it's too bad your father brought him in. Slim is hard to fool. On the other hand . . ." He shrugged.

"On the other hand, you don't mind a game of wits with a worthy opponent."

"That about says it."

She sighed. "I wish none of this had happened, but if anybody can get me out of this mess, you can." She spoke with quiet conviction.

Did he look pleased, at least for a moment? "Since you're in no position to judge," he reminded her, "I won't let that opinion go to my head."

Picking up a long stick, he poked at the fire. The sun was lowering over the western mountains and a chill was creeping into the air. "I suppose you're worried he'll find you and drag you back to your father."

"I . . . suppose so."

"Don't be. I won't let that happen. When you go back, it won't be on your daddy's say-so."

"Promise?"

Slowly he nodded his head, just once. It was enough. Jared Wolf did not offer promises lightly. All at once Lark felt safe and protected.

And then he added a single word. "But—"

She gasped, a little prickle of apprehension running down her spine.

"Sooner or later you'll have to face him, stand up to him. If you're ever going to lead your own life, you'll have to slug it out with him. And the longer you put it off, the harder it's going to be."

"I know you're right." Miserably she drew herself up, wrapping her arms around her knees and hunching her shoulders. "But I've already put it off for... for years. It's hard—"

"The hell it is. You just do it. You look the bastard in the eye and say, 'It's my life, dammit! Let me live it.'"

She gave a rueful little laugh. "Easy for you to say. You know who you are and where you belong. You've stayed in the mountains and made a simple life for yourself, one you love and that fits you perfectly. You've turned your back on all the things that most people strive for—money, prestige, power."

"I may not be the simple mountain man you take me for." He shifted on his blanket and stared into the flames.

"I didn't mean 'simple' as in not-too-bright," she said, amused. "You're the most complicated man I've ever known, and the most honest."

When he made no response, she continued hesitantly. "You're always so very sure of yourself. While I...I'm never sure of anything. If I had my life to live over, I'd do almost everything differently. I'm not surprised my father's disappointed in me because I'm...disappointed in myself."

She felt a tear slide down her cheek at precisely the same moment she felt his arm slide around her shoulders.

"Forget all that," he said roughly. "Forget your father and Slim Dugan and the rest of the civilized world. For a few days at least, it'll be just the two of us."

Tilting her chin, he kissed her.

Yes, she thought, her heart lifting, this is right, no matter what the future holds.

She shivered, and he drew her more fully, more safely, into his arms.

CHAPTER NINE

THAT night she lay in his arms beneath a star-littered sky on a mattress of evergreen boughs—in separate sleeping bags. The slightest movement sent a fresh burst of aromatic pine rising around them, until she was drunk with it—and with longing.

He'd kissed her good-night and tucked her into her own sleeping bag and she hadn't had the courage to make the first move. Still, she comforted herself, she lay beside him and would awaken in the morning curled in her own little cocoon inside the haven of his arms.

It would have to be enough.

For the next four days they drifted through the wilderness, camping each evening in a new location. They took their time, moving slowly and carefully. Finally he had time to answer her multitude of questions. So much of what he'd learned growing up here was foreign and wonderful to her.

How to tell direction by using the sun or moon or any star...how to read animal tracks...how to tie a proper knot and build a proper fire. Everything he taught or told her came as a revelation; she'd never even been a Girl Scout.

But quickly she learned how to prepare a meal of freeze-dried vegetables and a freshly caught trout; how to eat, without gagging, the roots and berries he harvested along the way; how to boil coffee in an old

145

blackened pot on the edge of a wood fire; and how to set a bent-branch snare—although she was relieved when her trap turned up empty.

And she began to learn how to walk more quietly through the forest, how to listen and how to see, *really* see what she looked at. Their meandering path led by Lookout Point and that night they gazed at the stars through Jared's telescope; they crossed shallow streams and meadows carpeted in wildflowers; they explored an old abandoned mine and even watched beavers building a dam.

It was all so heady and exciting that Lark's confidence grew by leaps and bounds—almost as fast as her admiration for her guide in this strange new world.

Even when he left her alone by Wolf Springs on the fifth day, she waved goodbye with perfect composure. He'd be back. She had nothing to worry about—and a nice, warm soak was just what she needed.

"He ain't gonna leave until he talks to her."

Jared, hunkered down on one side of a small fire, looked at Slim Dugan hunkered down on the other. Each man held a tin cup of coffee, poured from the metal pot suspended over the flames by forked sticks.

"She left of her own free will."

Slim shrugged, the expression on his bearded face uncaring. "Maybe so. He prefers thinkin' you drug his little gal off, or at least brainwashed her into goin'." A sarcastic spark lightened his eyes. "You havin' a good time up there, hoss?" He cast a knowing eye toward the high country.

Jared laughed. "Good enough," he admitted. "How long's Mallory prepared to wait this out?"

"All year, if it comes to that." Slim tossed down a slug of coffee. "Although it ain't exactly convenient. Man's got other problems."

"Oh?" Jared sloshed coffee around in his cup in a show of disinterest, although every sense had sprung to alert. "How so?"

Slim shrugged bony shoulders. "Somethin' about 'co-mingling of funds,' what the hell ever that is. That ol' boy sure don't want it known, and he's sweatin' bullets. But he ain't goin' nowhere until he talks to his girl."

The old mountain man's expression turned sly. "He ain't a very lovable sort, and that's the truth, but she's his soft spot. Now me, I'm gettin' a little tired of chasin' you two through the brush. If I had my druthers, I'd druther take my money and go on home."

"I see your point." Co-mingling of funds...and a multimillion-dollar headquarters complex under construction, as Jared had made it his business to know. *Bingo!*

"All I'm suggestin' is that you let me get close enough to give that girl her daddy's message. Then the two a'you can go jump off Wolf's Head Pass, for all I care."

Jared considered. Letting Slim speak to Lark wouldn't do a damned bit of good. It would only frighten her more to learn her father intended to stay until hell froze over, if that's what it took.

Maybe it was time to bring this impasse to a head while he was still in control, Jared thought—assuming he still was. "I've got a better idea," he said.

Slim nodded. "Thought you might. Let me hear it, hoss. Let me hear it...."

Lark slung her pack onto her back with all the finesse of an experienced mountaineer. "So where are we headed today?" she asked. "North, east, south—"

"West."

She straightened to attention. "But isn't that—?"

He nodded. "Civilization," he confirmed. "We need supplies and the Mountain Mom 'n' Pop Store is our best bet."

For a few moments she stood perfectly still. "That means he's still at the cabin. Otherwise, we'd just go there."

He said nothing, just looked at her with a narrow, thoughtful expression.

"How do you know?" Her voice rose. "You haven't been back there, have you? I mean, we haven't been separated long enough for you to get there and back."

"I just know, that's all."

"Jared, don't do this to me."

"Don't do what, Lark?" He met her anxious gaze, his own steady.

"Don't start holding out on me. I don't think I could stand it. We've gotten so close these last few weeks...." She sucked in a quick breath. "Is that it? Have we gotten too close for *your* comfort? Oh, Jared—"

Dropping the backpack, she cupped his face in her hands. The time had come to say what she had resisted saying for so long. She didn't know how she knew this was the crucial moment, but she did.

So she said simply, "I love you, Jared. I loved you before we left the cabin and I love you more now. Whatever happens, I'll always love you."

Something flickered in the depths of his dark eyes, flickered but failed to break through. "But do you trust me?"

She didn't even have to think about that. "With my life," she said simply.

"Then believe this, I'll do what's best for all of us." He lifted her pack and offered it to her.

She took it. Surely he would not betray her now. Surely not...

Lark and Jared moved together quickly and quietly through trees and across meadows. Neither spoke, as if what had been set in motion must play out in its own way.

The air was fresh and clean following a midday thunderstorm, which they'd waited out from the shelter of a cave. Now Lark found herself concentrating on her surroundings as if she could store up the wonder and beauty of what she had learned and experienced in these mountains.

But that was silly, she berated herself. Tonight they'd still be here just as they'd been for... how long now? She didn't know the date, had no idea what day of the week it might be. They'd been living in a different reality: eating when they were hungry, sleeping when they were tired, traveling when the spirit moved them.

He stopped short and she, who had been day-dreaming, ran into his broad back. "There." He pointed.

The Mountain Mom 'n' Pop Store lay at the bottom of the ridge beside a narrow dirt road which led higher toward Wolf Cabin.

Her heart stopped beating and she stared at the log structure, then at him. For an instant their glances locked, but his was closed and unreadable. He took her arm, leading her down the steep slope. She went meekly but her tension increased with every step.

Only one car stood in the dusty parking area. They walked past it and onto the wooden porch. Jared pushed open the front door and entered first, then held the door for her.

She followed so hesitantly that he gave her a sharp glance before turning toward the cheerful woman behind the counter in the middle of the room.

"Good to see you, Jared." She came forward to greet him. "Need a few things, do you?"

Jared nodded. "A few. Some matches and a can of—"

He followed her toward the back of the room. Lark started after him but a hand settled over her shoulder, stopping her in her tracks.

"Hello, Lark."

Her father, his voice trembling slightly, but whether from love or worry or anger or disappointment she could not guess. Her frantic gaze sought Jared but he stood across the room with his back toward her. Hadn't he heard? Didn't he know?

He had abandoned her to her worst nightmare. Slowly she turned, bracing herself. "H-hello, Father."

For a moment Drake Mallory stared at her; then he grabbed her in a bear hug that crushed the breath from her lungs. "Oh, Lark, Lark," he crooned. "I've been worried sick about you, little girl."

She would not return his embrace but neither could she pull away. When he straightened, she just stood there meeting his gaze. She felt completely drained, this meeting somehow anticlimactic.

"I told you not to worry," she said stiffly.

"No way in hell I wouldn't worry." He seemed to check himself, calm down before going on. "Wesley sends his love, and Risa, too."

She shivered beneath her heavy load of guilt. "Does Wes forgive me for breaking our engagement?"

"He forgives you for running off like that. The engagement . . ." Drake Mallory's glance skittered off to one side. "That's still on. Risa and I knew once you got this craziness out of your system, you'd come back. We wanted you to be able to do that without too much embarrassment."

She stared at him. "My goodness," she whispered, "you just don't listen, do you? My life has changed, Father. I'm with Jared Wolf, now, and I'm staying with him for as long as he'll let me."

Drake Mallory's fleshy face quivered and he let out a derisive snort. "Dammit, Lark, you've got the worst judgment of anybody I've ever dealt with. Jared Wolf!" He practically spit out the name. "If that's all that stands between you and your fiancé, a good man who's loved you all your life, then we haven't got a damned thing to worry about!"

She stiffened. "Don't start," she warned in a steely tone. "I love Jared Wolf and I'm not going to let you—"

"Let me, hell!" Drake rammed both big hands through the salt and pepper hair. His expression grew calmer, slyer. "You know he set you up."

"W-what?"

"Set you up! Sold you down the river. Made a fool of you—whatever you want to call it. This meeting was Jared Wolf's doing. Tell her, Dugan."

She hadn't even noticed Slim Dugan, loitering in the background, or if she had, it hadn't registered. She should have. He was exactly as she remembered, even more as Jared had described him, down to the hard, indifferent eyes.

"Shore." Dugan shrugged. "All I wanted was a chance to give you a message but Wolf suggested a meeting instead. No big deal or nothin'."

Maybe not to him, but to her it was a very big deal indeed.

Her father added quickly, "That Wolf boy's had it in for me for years. My girls are my weakness and he knows that. After he called Wes—"

"Jared called Wes? He *spoke* to Wes?" A pit seemed to open beneath her feet.

"That's right. Hell, his revenge wouldn't be complete until he rubbed our noses in it. He's no good, never was. When he tried his funny stuff with Risa, it didn't work, but you—you're not as sharp about these things as she is, and—"

"Wait, wait." Lark flung up her hands. "What are you talking about? Risa and Jared? I know she went out with him a time or two but that was years ago."

Drake Mallory patted her shoulder, at the same time managing to step closer, until he blotted out her view of Jared at the opposite end of the store. "Sweetheart, you're the second Mallory that bastard has tried to...mess with. Risa saw through him and gave him his walking papers but somehow he's managed to pull the wool over your eyes. Little girl, you're too good to see the bad in people."

The hate-filled glance he aimed at the back of the room sent shivers down Lark's spine. She knew too well that Jared's antipathy was equally strong. What better way to get revenge than by sleeping with his enemy's daughter—and then rubbing everybody's nose in it?

But she couldn't believe that! She and Jared had been through too much together. "You're wrong," she whispered. "Don't say any more!" She pressed her hands over her ears. "Jared is good, he's honest. I've been happier here with him than I even dreamed possible. Here things are simple and clean and—"

"There's nothing simple about it." Drake bared his teeth in a derisive grimace. "A man with as much money and as many responsibilities as Jared Wolf's got—"

"M-money? He hasn't got any money." She glanced at Slim Dugan but no gesture of support was forthcoming from that quarter.

Drake thought he had her now; it was there in his triumphant expression. "Little girl, don't you know? He owns his own multimillion-dollar company. Wolf Cache Systems, I believe it's called. Has to do with storage systems for computers, something like that."

"No." She glanced at Dugan. The faintest narrowing of his eyes told her that this time what her father said was true. Jared Wolf wasn't an itinerant mountain man, he was a wealthy entrepreneur. She should have known; she should have known. But still, the last faint flicker of hope remained, refused to die.

Her father took her elbow. "Let me take you home, Lark, take care of you like I always have. I know what's best for you, baby."

His words made her scalp crawl. He'd taken care of her, all right, to the point where her entire identity was tied up in being his daughter.

She backed away from him, out of his grasp. "Where's Jared? I've got to talk to Jared."

"I'm right here, Lark."

The sound of that much-loved voice was almost her undoing. It took every ounce of strength not to throw herself into his arms and beg him to take her away from here. But she must be strong just this once . . . be brave, as he himself had so often advised her.

She drew a shaky breath. "You're rich?" It was a question and a statement, all at once.

He shrugged. "Rich is a relative term."

"You own your own company?"

"Yes."

"Why didn't you tell me?"

"Because you didn't want to know."

"I didn't—?" She frowned.

"That's right. You were here for the mountain thing, the fantasy. I let you have it."

What other fantasies had he allowed her? "Did . . . did you call Wes?"

"Yes."

"Jared!" She clenched her hands at her sides in an agony of disappointment. "Why didn't you tell me?"

"Because..." his dark gaze slashed toward Drake Mallory "...then I'd have had to confront you for lying to me. It just didn't seem worth it, Goldilocks."

"But I don't understand."

"Hell, it's simple." His lip curled. "You swore to me you'd called off your engagement, then conveniently forgot to inform the poor slob waiting back in Florida."

"But I can explain that! Can *you* explain deliberately going behind my back to let everyone know where I was so you could hurt my father?" She couldn't go on, couldn't accuse him of sleeping with her only for revenge.

For a moment he just stared at her as if he'd never seen her before. Then he shrugged. "Trust is a two-way street, Lark. I won't explain and I won't deny. You either meant the things you said to me or you didn't. You either trust me or you don't."

And he turned and walked away.

Now she knew why he had never told her he loved her, even after she finally said the words to him.

Because he didn't.

He'd used her to get even with her father and perhaps her sister, as well. Now he was through with her. Thank goodness, she hadn't told him about her father's business problems!

She looked down at the wooden floor, at the scarred toes of her hiking boots, at the shiny toes of her father's expensive shoes. With great effort, she forced her gaze up to her father's face.

If he'd looked sly or triumphant, it might have given her the impetus she needed to turn away from him. But instead he looked worn and haggard, and for the first time she realized that he had suffered, too.

He spoke heavily. "Rebellion doesn't suit you, little girl. Let's go home."

Home. Apparently that was the only choice left for her. And yet— Her glance skittered around the room, seeking Jared, but he was gone.

Lark discovered that her absence had not brought wedding plans to a screeching halt as she'd supposed—had not, in fact, even slowed them down appreciably. On her first day back, Risa arrived like a minor tornado, flinging files and notes and samples around the bedroom in her rush to throw her arms around the prodigal sister.

"I was so worried," Risa whispered, kissing Lark's cheek. She stepped back with assessing eyes that widened in astonishment. "But, Lark! I don't believe that after all you've been through, you can look so wonderful. You've gained a few pounds and the dark circles are gone from beneath your eyes."

Lark shrugged. She didn't care how she looked. She didn't care about much of anything, a conscious decision and all that kept her from collapsing into a little puddle of tears. She let Risa draw her down on a love seat near the window. Through the pane she saw a wide white beach and the gray Atlantic, instead of towering green mountains.

Risa went on in a gently reproving tone. "So you were in Colorado the whole time."

Lark nodded. "I didn't know Father had sold the cabin."

Risa's brows rose. "Did he? I just thought we stopped going there." She cleared her throat. "Ah . . . you were with Jared Wolf?"

Lark jumped up, the mere mention of his name causing the first crack in her outward composure. "I don't want to talk about him."

"I don't blame you." Risa looked grim. "There's nothing to be gained by getting into it, I suppose. But we do have to talk about Wes."

Lark knew that was true but she couldn't hold back the groan. "Wes! Surely everyone understands I can't marry him now. Not after . . ."

Not after Jared; not after loving and losing. What a fool she'd been to think it better to love and lose than never to love at all. But love she had, and it had put her feelings for Wes into stark relief. She liked him; she respected him; she'd never love him as she now knew herself capable of loving, not if she tried for a million years.

Risa slipped an arm around Lark's trembling shoulders. "Father did a masterful job of keeping this quiet. Practically the entire world still expects you to become Mrs. Wesley Sherborn in slightly less than a week. You may have more options than you realize, dear. Don't make any decisions until you speak to him."

Lark closed her eyes. The thought of confessing her true feelings to Wes almost made her ill, but she owed him that much. "You're right."

"Good, because here he is."

At Risa's brisk announcement, Lark opened her eyes to find that the door to her bedroom stood wide, revealing her erstwhile fiancé, a bouquet of roses in his hand and an uncertain expression on his face.

Risa edged toward the door. She looked on the verge of collapse herself, Lark thought. One more person who's suffered because I'm such a wimp, she berated herself. It's no wonder Father thinks me incapable of making an intelligent decision. Well, that's in the past.

The door closed and Lark found herself alone with Wes. Blond and polished and civilized in his pastel shirt and trousers, he was the very antithesis of—

"These are for you." He thrust the flowers in her general direction.

"Thank you." She accepted the bouquet.

"I'm glad you're back."

"Why?"

"Because . . ." He frowned, looking genuinely confused. "We're getting married in six days, remember?"

She clutched the flowers so tightly that a thorn bit into one fingertip. "You can't still want to marry me, not after—"

"I do," he said quickly. "I love you, Lark."

She would have given almost anything not to hear those words. *I hate you* would have eased her guilty conscience, because that's what she deserved. "I love you, too, Wes." She spoke carefully, wanting to make sure he understood exactly what she meant. "But I'm not sure it's the kind of love it takes to make a marriage work. I think it's more a case of knowing each other forever, and of our families pushing us into something that may not be . . . in our best interests."

She didn't really expect him to understand what she was trying to say. Wes wasn't exactly known for great depth; he tended to brush off subtleties or miss them entirely.

This time he surprised her. "You met someone else in Colorado?"

"Yes." She faced him squarely, surprised to discover that she wasn't ashamed of loving Jared, only sorry it hadn't worked out.

"Are you going to marry him?"

"No." Not a chance in the world of that happening.

"You're sure?"

"I'm sure."

"Then are you planning to spend the rest of your life alone?"

"I . . . I don't—no, at least I hope not. But it's still too painful to think about the future."

"Dammit, Lark!"

She'd never known Wes to speak with such frustration, and she looked at him in shocked surprise.

He stomped across the room to the window and stared out. "Do you think you're the only one who's ever suffered from unrequited love?"

"You mean, you—"

He gave a bitter little laugh. "Yeah. She's not available, end of story. And then we've got you, dumped by your mountain man."

She'd take "dumped" over "betrayed" any day.

"Then what do we have to lose?" He whirled away from the window and grabbed her elbows, nearly lifting her off her feet. "My folks want this marriage, your father wants this marriage. Hell, I'm never going to love another woman the way I love her but it's never going to work out."

He'd used the present tense: *love*. For a fleeting moment, Lark wondered who the woman might be, not that it mattered.

He continued grimly. "I don't intend to spend the rest of my life alone. If I tried, I'd go crazy—just like you will, if you don't get out of this house for good."

God, that was the truth. "So you think we should go ahead with the wedding?" She could hardly believe he'd suggest such a thing.

"That's right." A muscle ridged in his jaw. "Good marriages have been built on less than mutual respect. We have that, at least. So I'm asking you again, Lark—this time without witnesses so you can turn me down if you want to. Will you marry me?"

His smile flashed; so his first proposal *had* been staged to preclude a refusal. She'd thought so all along, but he'd seemed so ingenuous at the time.

She was finding unsuspected depths to him. But could she marry him?

He waited, not pushing, letting her decide on her own. But she needed one more answer.

"I understand…Jared called you on the phone and that's how everyone knew where I'd gone."

He hesitated for a long moment before nodding. "That's right."

His reply swept away any last, faint hope she might have harbored about Jared's part in all this. Everything he'd done, he'd done for revenge, and she might as well face it. Still, she could rob him of his final victory, the one thing above all others that would hurt Drake Mallory.

She looked up into Wes Sherborn's blue eyes and said in a voice filled with new determination, "Yes, Wes. My answer is yes. I'll marry—"

The rest was lost in his embrace. Only later, as he slipped the diamond engagement ring back on her finger, did she discover that a rose thorn had pricked her breast above her heart, leaving a tiny telltale dot of crimson on the ivory-colored silk.

In the pain of the moment, she hadn't even noticed.

Emerging from Lark's bedroom, they found both Drake and Risa hovering in the hall, waiting anxiously to learn the outcome of their meeting.

"Well?" Drake demanded. "Is it on or off?"

Wes slipped an arm around Lark's waist and grinned. "On."

Lark's father slumped. "Thank God." Straightening, he grabbed Wes's hand and pumped it vigorously. "You've made the right decision, kids. All that's happened in the last few weeks—hell, by the time your first anniversary rolls around you won't even remember it."

Risa, her eyes glittering with tears, hugged the bride-to-be. "I'm so relieved," she whispered. "I'm sure you're doing the right thing and that you'll both be very happy."

Lark returned the hug, wishing she could be half as sure as everyone else seemed to be.

August twenty-sixth, twenty-seventh, twenty-eighth... The countdown to August thirtieth passed in a haze for Lark. Feigning enthusiasm, she let herself be swept along by the enthusiasm of others.

Everyone seemed so sure that she could only gather her guilt more closely around her and smile and smile and try to put her Colorado misadventure behind her. But every night before she fell asleep, the things that had happened to her in the mountains played behind her closed lids like movies in a darkened theater. And Jared was always there, the star.

But he had never loved her. He'd used her. When he thought of her now, he must laugh at her gullibility.

She hadn't even provided him with a decent challenge.

Jenny Wolf slammed a glass of lemonade on the table in front of Jared. "How can you be so stubborn!" she cried.

In his high chair, Little Jared stopped eating and stared at his mother with surprise, then went back to feeding himself applesauce—messily.

Jared curved one hand around his glass. "Mind your own business, Jen."

Jenny sat down in the chair across from him. "But she's getting married in two days—*two days*! You've got to stop her!"

"It's none of my business. Yours, either." He gulped half the contents of the glass. "That boy of yours is really growing."

"Don't try to change the subject." Jenny drummed her fingernails on the oak tabletop. "Tell me what happened that last day, Jared. I can't believe she really left with her father after—"

"After what?" he asked quickly.

Jenny shrugged. "After what she told me about him, the way he's always bullied her. It took a lot of guts for her to run away from Florida in the first place. To go meekly back just because he came after her—" She shook her head. "It just doesn't make any sense, unless..."

"Unless what?"

"Unless you let her down in some way. Jared, I shouldn't say this—"

"Then don't." He stood up abruptly. "Look, I've got to get to Denver. I'm selling Wolf Cache Systems and I've got business to take care of."

She jumped to her feet and darted around the table to block his exit. "You need to hear this." She grabbed him by the shoulders and hung on. "That girl loves you. She would never have left if you'd lifted your little finger to stop her. So why didn't you?"

"You've got it all wrong, Jenny." He spoke softly, each word distinct. "Her old man convinced her that I used her, then betrayed her as part of an elaborate scheme of revenge."

Jenny looked dumbfounded. "And she took his word over yours?"

"Not exactly." He shook her hands aside and stepped back. "Do you really think I'd stand there arguing with that bastard Mallory, fighting over her like she was some kind of prize?" He shoved his hair back from his face with both hands. "If she gave a damn about me, she'd have trusted me instead of him, no matter how it looked. All she had to do was show a little faith."

He had never seen an expression quite like the one that appeared on his sister's face. It looked almost like . . . pity.

"She loves you," Jenny said with finality. "She told me so, and I'll bet she told you, too."

Jared shrugged. "Sure. What of it?"

"Did you ever say those words to her?"

"Hell, Jen, we said a lot of words to each other, some of them true."

"Don't be evasive, Jared Wolf. Did you ever tell Lark Mallory that you loved her?"

His silence provided an answer. Jenny nodded slowly. "And you talk about trust and faith," she said, her disappointment, like her tone, clear and cutting. "You ask a lot, Jared, but it seems to me you're prepared to give very little."

And as he walked away, he heard her call after him, "Think about it, Jared. Just think about it...."

CHAPTER TEN

AUGUST 30th.

Lark's wedding day dawned hot and clear. Standing in her bedroom window watching the sun come up over the Atlantic, she forced deep, even breaths into her lungs in an attempt to calm herself.

Last night she'd dreamed again of the mountains....

Stop! she commanded herself. Jared never cared for her even the least bit. She mustn't let him intrude on this day of all days for if she did, she'd never be able to do what must be done.

She'd just stepped from the shower when Risa arrived. Lark took one look at her sister and for the moment, at least, forgot her own troubles.

"Something's wrong," she said. "Risa, what is it?"

Risa chewed at her lower lip. "Nothing. Nothing at all."

"But you look . . . I guess the word is . . . *weak*. Are you feeling all right? Are you ill?"

"Of course not. I'm just . . ." Risa gulped and her eyes opened wide. "I . . . I—"

Clasping one hand over her mouth, she made a dash for the bathroom, slamming the door in Lark's face when she would have followed. Leaning against that barrier, Lark heard the unmistakable sounds of barfing.

She pounded on the door. "Risa! Let me in this minute! *Risa!*"

Dragging footsteps, then the snick of the lock and the door swung open. Risa, pale and wan, stood there with drooping head. Lark started forward but Risa took a hasty step back.

"Don't! Don't touch me, please."

"Then tell me what it is!" Wild with concern, Lark twisted her hands together to keep from grabbing her sister in a protective embrace which obviously wasn't wanted.

Risa walked out of the bathroom and to the bed, where she leaned weakly against a tall footpost. "I didn't want you to know until after you got back from your honeymoon. I thought I'd be able to keep it from you but I hadn't taken into account how early I'd need to get here on your wedding day."

Suddenly she turned, her chin lifting defensively. "I'm pregnant, Lark. Morning sickness—that's all it is."

Enormous relief poured through Lark, quickly followed by joy. "Risa, that's wonderful! I'm so happy for you."

"Th-*thank* you!" Risa's face crumpled and she collapsed on the edge of the bed in a storm of tears.

Tears of happiness, Lark thought, until her sister looked up and cried, "*Now what am I going to do?*"

Lark settled Risa in a comfortable chair and rang for a pot of decaffeinated coffee and a plate of sweet rolls. By the time the tray arrived, Risa had regained at least nominal control of herself. Lark accepted the refreshments and managed to get the door closed without anyone the wiser.

"Now," she said, pouring coffee for them both. "Tell me what's going on. I thought you wanted children."

Risa sniffed and dabbed at her nose with a tissue. Seated in the big chair, wearing no makeup and with her legs curled beneath her, she looked much younger than her thirty years—younger and more vulnerable.

"Of course I want children," she said, her voice shaky. "I just don't . . . I don't want them with Tony! Oh, Lark, I shouldn't be telling you this on your wedding day."

Lark couldn't have been more shocked if Risa had announced she planned to swim the English Channel. "But I thought— You and Tony seem—"

"Well, we *have* to, don't we?" Risa swallowed hard. "Remember just before you took off, when I told you someday I'd tell you about *my* wedding day?"

"Yes, but I thought you were just trying to cheer me up."

"Well, I was, in that I never really expected I'd be telling you what actually happened. But I'm to the point where I've got to talk to someone or I'll go completely out of my mind."

Coming from Risa, sensible, self-confident Risa, that was quite an admission. Lark reached out to squeeze her sister's hand, ashamed she'd been so wrapped up in her own misery that she hadn't seen what was under her nose. "Honey, I'll be glad to listen. I'm not sure I'll be able to come up with any good advice but at least I'm here."

Risa's lips trembled. "Thanks. I knew I could count on you." She steadied herself. "You know Tony had the Father Seal of Approval, right?"

"Well, yes. I know he always liked Tony."

"Liked. Ha! Tony was hand-picked by Daddy dearest. At first I didn't mind—I mean, he's handsome, ambitious, got a great future. But he's also possessive and overbearing and takes me for granted. That's why we broke up."

"You broke up? When? I had no idea. I thought once you and Tony got together, it was smooth sailing."

"It wasn't." Risa pleated her napkin into a fan shape, her fingers visibly trembling. "There was someone else...."

Lark's heart sank. "Someone Father disapproved of?"

"He never figured out who it was, thank God. If he had—" She shuddered. "He just knew I was digging in my heels when he tried to shove me at Tony. The more I held back, the harder he pushed. I thought I could stand up to him...but I was wrong. God, I was so wrong!" She covered her face with her hands for a moment, breathing hard. Then she squared her shoulders and lifted her tear-stained face.

"Oh, Risa." Lark wished she had the words of comfort that her sister needed so much to hear. "I'm so sorry. What can I do?"

"There's nothing anyone can do, now that I'm... pregnant." She said the word on a groan. "I want children, I really do. I know I'll love this child, but I also know that now I'm tied to this marriage forever. Before, there was always the hope, however far-fetched, that someday I'd get up the nerve...."

"To leave Tony?"

"To leave Father! But we both know how hard that is."

Lark watched great tears well in her sister's eyes. "Do you still see the man you love from time to time?"

"Yes." It was the merest whisper of sound. "He still cares for me, too, which makes it even worse. If only I'd had the courage to do what I knew was right. But we both had other obligations and we...we thought we'd get over it...."

At least I'm better off than that, Lark thought. Jared never cared for me at all, so it's not as if I could win him back if I had the courage to try.

All courage would get her was the prospect of a life even lonelier than the one she saw stretching out before her now. She still wouldn't have the man she loved, and she'd also forfeit her family and the only life she'd ever known.

"Is there anything I can do for you," Lark pleaded, "anything at all?"

Tears streaked Risa's pale cheeks. "Just be happy, Lark. Make Wes happy. You both deserve it."

Lark no longer knew *what* she deserved.

Karen Dodd, the long-suffering wedding consultant, smoothed the satin gown over Lark's hips with a murmur of approval.

"Fits like a glove," she pronounced. "I can't believe it—this is incredible work. When you came back from that beauty farm with an extra ten pounds—oh, I'm sorry!" The flustered woman recoiled. "Not that you didn't need them, because you did. I meant to say, ten more pounds than you left with, after we'd already altered this dress three times in the other direction."

Lark smiled at the hapless woman. "I understood perfectly what you meant. It had to be frustrating, being expected to let it out again."

"Exactly!"

Ms. Dodd shot a glance at Risa, sitting on the foot of the bed in her wedding-attendant lingerie. She looked pale but contained, her hands folded carefully in her lap.

Lark couldn't believe she was standing here wearing this wedding gown. During the weeks she'd spent in Colorado, she'd somehow managed to forget all about it. Now she was wearing it for real; the next time she took it off, she'd be a married woman.

A shock rippled through her at the realization.

A soft knock on the door interrupted her thoughts.

"The hairdresser and the beautician are here," a voice called. "Are you ready for them?"

"Come right in," Ms. Dodd invited. She secured the last tiny button on Lark's gown before turning to greet the newcomers, entering with boxes and totes and bags of supplies and equipment. "You—" she pointed "take care of the bride's hair while you—" pointing again "—can do the matron of honor's makeup. Let's go, let's go!" She clapped her hands sharply. "We don't want to leave anything to chance, now do we?"

No chance, Lark thought. None whatsoever.

Lark sat before her makeup mirror, watching the makeup artist paint and pat and smooth. He really *is* an artist, she acknowledged with a kind of detached admiration. *I don't look like the same woman who came dragging back only a few days ago.*

Risa stood to one side, her own transformation complete. She looked lovely, Lark thought admiringly. This genius had managed to completely eradicate the outward vestiges of inner turmoil.

Another knock on the door; there'd been a steady progression of telegrams, telephone calls, last-minute decisions and silly questions. In the mirror, Lark watched her sister walk to the door, speak to someone in the hall, then step outside and close the door.

"There!" The makeup man adjusted the layers of her veil, then stepped back and gave her a critical look. "You're gorgeous."

"No, you're a magician." Lark put all the enthusiasm she could muster into her voice.

He looked pleased. "True, too true. I *am* fabulous, but at least you gave me something to work with. As challenges go, you weren't." He paused in the act of gathering up materials, his hands filled with fluffy brushes and colorful pencils. "That's a compliment, by the way."

"That's how I took it," Lark assured him.

Risa reentered as the cosmetologist departed. She had an uncertain, almost furtive look about her.

Lark frowned. "What is it? What's happened now?"

Risa drew in a deep breath that strained the seams of her rose-colored gown. Looking heavenward, she muttered, "God, let me do the right thing."

Lark waited, although she didn't feel as if she could take much more emotional upheaval today—not and keep her sanity.

"Another wedding gift just arrived."

"Tell them to stick it in the solarium with everything else," Lark said. "Why on earth would they bother us with this now, when—?"

"Because of the way it's marked." Slowly she extracted something from the folds of her skirt, where she'd been clutching it in one hand: an envelope, a simple envelope. Hesitantly, she offered it to Lark.

Lark looked at the notation in red ink: *Important—Please deliver immediately*. There was no return address.

Her heart stopped beating. This envelope was from Jared Wolf, she knew that as surely as she knew the Rocky Mountains were still stand—

"W-what happened?"

"You almost fainted. My God, Lark, are you all right? Here, drink this water. Oh, dear, I'm afraid to even put a damp cloth on your face with your makeup already done and—"

Lark straightened in the chair where Risa had somewhere managed to deposit her. Trembling from head to foot, she looked down at the envelope still clutched in her hand. With clumsy fingers, she ripped it open and extracted something—some kind of legal paper.

She realized what she held in her hand and gasped.

Risa cried out in alarm. "You've gone as white as a sheet. What is it?"

Lark drew in a deep, steadying breath. "It's the deed to Wolf Cabin, and a note from Jared." Quickly she read: *I figure I owe you this, and more. I was too hard on you. You deserve every happiness and I hope you find it. Jared.*

He was giving her Wolf Cabin for a wedding gift.

Impossible; it couldn't be true. That cabin meant more to him than all the money in the world, all the...all the revenge in the world. That he would give it now to the daughter of his worst enemy could mean only one thing.

He loves me, she thought. *He loves me—he can't possibly deny it now. Whatever has happened, whatever he may have done, this is his way of telling me that he loves me.*

All her lethargy fell away. Grabbing Risa's hands, Lark cried, ''Tell me the truth! What happened between you and Jared Wolf all those years ago?''

Risa looked first surprised, then distinctly uncomfortable. ''Do I have to? It wasn't my finest hour.''

''Please. It's important.''

''If you say so.'' She sighed. ''It wasn't much, really. I chased him unmercifully, as you may or may not remember. I've always been attracted to the hard-to-get type and he wasn't having any, at least not for the first couple of years.''

''And then?''

''We went out a time or two that last summer. I had to sneak out to meet him after everyone was asleep, which was a drag. And it turned out that as a couple, we just didn't click. We'd pretty much called it quits by the time Father found out.'' She rolled her eyes. ''He caught me trying to sneak back into the cabin. Boy, did it ever hit the fan! Father blamed Jared entirely, of course. I'll never forget what he said—''

She clamped her lips together as if sorry she'd brought that up.

"Tell me. Please, I have to know."

Risa sighed. "Okay, but remember, you asked for it. He said no two-bit half-breed would ever lay hands on a daughter of his. Try it, he said, and the second thing he'd do was set a torch to that precious cabin Jared was so worried about. And then he said, 'You know what the first thing will be.'"

Lark's shoulders slumped; she could hardly believe this. On top of everything else, her father was a closet bigot. No wonder Jared, so proud of his heritage, despised Drake Mallory. She pressed on. "Father said something else . . . that Jared tried to 'mess with' you. Those were his exact words."

Risa laughed mirthlessly. "If there was any interest in 'messing,' it was coming from the other direction. Jared Wolf was always a perfect gentleman. I'm ashamed to say that I wasn't as perfect a lady. And I didn't even stand up for him when Father said all those horrible things. But that's only one of many regrets. If I had it to do over—"

She began to prowl around the room restlessly. "If I had it to do over, I wouldn't. I've made a horrible mess of things, Lark—my life, Tony's, and—" she placed one hand on her stomach "—this baby's, I don't doubt. I thought I was doing the right thing, placating Father. It was easier than fighting him, but now I see how much it's cost."

Lark touched her sister's hand. "There's one more thing I have to ask you, Risa."

"What more can I possibly tell you? I feel as if I've already bared my soul."

"Father said Jared called Wes and told him where I was. Is that true?" She knew the answer but felt obliged to grasp at straws.

Risa looked torn. "I wish you hadn't asked that, but since you did—yes, Jared called Wes. I don't know exactly what was said but he did call. Later that same day, Father left for Colorado to bring you home."

Faint with disappointment, Lark sat down heavily in the chair before the window. "Thank you for being honest," she said hoarsely. "W-would you mind giving me a few minutes alone before we leave for the church?"

Risa looked doubtful, but finally nodded. "I'll go downstairs and make sure the limousines are here," she said at last. "If you need me—"

"Thank you."

Lark watched her sister leave before turning to look out the window. Below, gardeners worked on the lawn and flower beds, manicuring everything to a state of artificial perfection. How different from what she'd grown to love in Colorado, just as the man she was to marry differed from the man she loved.

Yes, loved. Even if he had deceived her, she loved him still. There were many ways to rationalize that telephone call but she wouldn't stoop to any of them. What difference did it make, really? He loved her; she felt that with absolute certainty. Otherwise, he would never have sent her the deed to Wolf Cabin, the symbol of everything he held dear...would he?

Either he loved her or he was determined to eradicate everything that might remind him of the time they'd shared. Which was it? Should she stake her entire future, her very life, on the answer?

On an impulse, she hurried to the telephone beside her bed. It took a few minutes to get Jenny's telephone number, and then the ringing on the other end of the wire continued for so long Lark feared she'd struck out.

At last a breathless voice answered.

"Jenny! Thank God you're there."

"Lark, is that you? What's wrong? Isn't this your wedding day?"

"Yes, but— Jenny, where's Jared? I really, *really* need to talk to him."

"Why, I don't know. I mean, I've got no idea. He was by here a few days ago but I lit into him pretty hard and I haven't seen hide nor hair of him since."

"You lit into him? Why?"

An indelicate snort came across the wire. "Because he was being a jerk, that's why. He should never have let you go, Lark. I told him so."

Lark closed her eyes. "Thanks for trying. If I thought there was a chance he cared...."

"He cares." Jenny spoke with complete assurance. "Will he overcome that stubborn pride enough to admit it? I wish I could tell you he will, but I can't. He's my brother and I love him, but he's not a man who forgives. I'm sorry, Lark. I wish I could be more help but I can't encourage you to throw everything away on what would be an outside shot, at best."

"I... appreciate your honesty. Goodbye, Jenny."

"'Bye, Lark. Good luck."

She'd need it. Hanging up the telephone, Lark turned, her own reflection in the mirrored closet doors catching her attention. A flash of déjà vu hit her and she was back on the carpeted dais in the bridal shop in Palm Beach.

Only this was a different woman, outside as well as inside. Hollow cheeks and haunted eyes had made way for a glowing complexion and eyes that burned with fresh determination.

This new Lark Mallory was not going to be anybody's victim! That was the old Lark; this new one had the strength and determination to go after what she wanted, no matter what the odds. And what she wanted was Jared Wolf. For him, she'd—

She laughed out loud. She'd climb the highest mountain, if she had to, but he wasn't going to get away from her without a fight.

Lifting her heavy skirts, she strode to the door and threw it open. Ms. Dodd stood in the hallway, holding a clipboard upon which she was making notations.

"Ms. Mallory! You look fabulous. Wait here and I'll make sure the coast is clear before you go downstairs."

"That won't be necessary." Lark started toward the curving stairway at the end of the hall.

Ms. Dodd hurried after. "Stop! You don't understand. Your bridegroom was down there a few minutes ago, talking to your father. You know it's bad luck for the groom to see the bride before the ceremony. Please, Ms. Mallory, stop!"

But Lark didn't. Lifting the voluminous skirt knee-high, she skimmed down the stairs, her legs a blur in sheer pale stockings and white satin slippers. She reached the marble-floored foyer just in time to catch a glimpse of a formally clad figure exiting through the heavy front door.

"Wes!" Racing to the door, she flung it open. Wes paused on the broad front steps, turning in obvious surprise.

"Lark!" He glanced around uncertainly. "Am I supposed to see you now?"

"You've *got* to see me now. We need to talk." She gestured urgently toward the house. "Come back inside for a minute, please? This is important."

"It must be."

He followed her into the library where she closed the door. Squaring her shoulders, she faced him.

"My God," he breathed. "I've never seen you look so beautiful. Your eyes sparkle and you just—" You just glow."

She found his compliment curiously embarrassing, since the attributes he'd just described were the result of her love for another man. Her engagement ring slid off her finger as if it had never belonged there in the first place. Wordlessly, she held it out to him.

He stared at her, making no move to take the diamond. "What's this?"

"I can't go through with the wedding, Wes. I'm sorry. Everything you said before is true, but only to a point. Respect and friendship might be enough to build a marriage, but not when the person you really love is alive and well and living in Colorado."

He seemed to reel with the shock. "You mean that Wolf guy? You really love him?"

"With all my heart and soul."

"And you think there's a chance you can get together with him? You didn't think so before."

"While there's life, there's hope. At the very least I've got to try."

He looked at her with a kind of sad disbelief. "Drake said it was just a passing infatuation. He said the guy didn't give a damn about you, was just using you for revenge."

"That's not true."

"I told you how your father found you, right? Because this Jared Wolf called me."

She nodded, not trusting her voice.

After a moment's hesitation, Wes sighed. "Look, Drake told me—hell, he warned me not to tell you this but I'm going to, anyway. You've got a right to know, now that you've made up your mind."

"W-what?" For the first time she wavered. What fresh disaster was about to overtake her?

"Jared Wolf didn't deliberately betray you. In retrospect, I think he was trying to find out if the wedding was on or off. When I told him it was on, he asked for an address where he could send a wedding present. I gave it to him. I had no idea who he was until later, when I mentioned his name to your father. Drake went ballistic. That's how it happened, Lark."

At that moment, she loved Wes Sherborn. Rising on tiptoe, she gave him a quick hug and a kiss on the cheek. "Thank you for telling me that," she cried. "I'd made up my mind but now I know for sure that I'm doing the right thing. All I have to do is find him—"

"Good luck," he called after her as she ran through the doorway. "Although somehow I don't think you'll need it."

Which turned out to be a self-fulfilling prophecy as she slammed into a tall figure just entering the foyer from outside. He caught her in his arms and held her against his chest, and she didn't have to see his face to know who'd come to her rescue—again.

"Jared!" she cried. "Oh, Jared, I—"

"Shut up." He kissed her soundly. Raising his head, he glared down at her. "I've come to get you," he said fiercely. "You'll never run away again, Lark. That's all over."

She clung to him. "Aren't you forgetting something?"

"What, that you're standing here in your wedding gown about to marry someone else? I've got to admit, I had a problem with that. But someday the guy'll thank me for bringing you to your senses before it was too late."

"The guy's already thanking you."

At the sound of Wes's voice, Jared's arms clenched so tightly around Lark that she thought he'd bruise a rib. Jared stared over the top of her head at his former rival, dark eyes hooded.

Wes gave a lopsided little grin. "I'd rather face the embarrassment of a church full of people expecting a wedding than try to make a go of a marriage doomed before it began."

Jared gave a curt nod. "It took you a while, Sherborn, but you finally caught on." He tugged Lark toward the door. "Let's go."

"Not yet." She resisted the steady pull. "You're still forgetting something."

"Dammit, Lark—"

Wes raised his brows and spoke directly to Jared. "And you thought *I* was slow," he muttered, turning to stroll nonchalantly down the hall with hands in the pockets of his striped pants.

Jared frowned, then looked down at the woman in his arms. Instantly the frown disappeared, replaced by a broad smile. "I love you," he said triumphantly. "Is *that* what you're waiting to hear?"

"Yes!"

She flung herself at him and he swept her off her feet. Clutching her against his chest, he carried her through the doorway and sprinted toward the rental car double-parked in the curving driveway crowded with limousines, their drivers loitering nearby under a cloud of cigarette smoke.

Her satin train trailed after them, her long veil floated like gossamer in their wake. After a surprised glance, the little knot of drivers burst into instantaneous applause cut off by a roar of outrage from the house.

Drake Mallory rushed out into the marble steps, shaking a fist after the fleeing couple. "Damn you, Jared Wolf, you bring my little girl back! I'll have you up on kidnapping charges, I swear I will! You can't come in here and—"

Lark, her arms tight around Jared's neck, didn't cower before her father's wrath this time. Instead she gave him the words Jared had urged her to say. "It's my life, dammit! Let me live it!"

Jared, shaking with laughter, flung open the passenger door and deposited her inside. Whipping around the front, he jumped into the driver's seat while Lark rolled down the window and leaned out.

She'd lost a father, to her regret, but she'd gained the love of her life. Perhaps someday the two men would reconcile. Until that day came—if it ever did—she'd continue to hope for a miracle.

Jared started the engine. "Ready?" he asked, looking at her with an expression of love and pride on his face.

"For anything," she promised. As the vehicle started forward, she saw her father still standing in the entryway, his shoulders slumped as if he'd finally realized he'd lost.

Leaning out of the window, she cried, "I love you, Father, but *I'm not your little girl anymore!*"

She was a woman—Jared Wolf's woman.

Forever, if not longer....

EPILOGUE

Two years from the day Lark Mallory Wolf ran away for the very last time, she found herself receiving callers in a Denver hospital. The occasion was one of great joy, for she'd just given birth to a beautiful eight-pound, two-ounce baby boy. Her handsome and much beloved husband, who'd sold his company and returned to his family trade of ranching, was at her side.

Her sister-in-law Jenny was the baby's first visitor. She came bearing gifts and a message from four-year-old Little Jared, declaring himself delighted at the prospect of having a *boy* cousin to play with.

Holding her husband's hand, Lark told herself that she was surely the happiest woman in the world.

With only a couple of exceptions....

The first was her sister, Risa, who'd lost her own baby and then gone through a painful divorce. Lark hadn't really expected Risa to fly all the way to Colorado to be reminded of her sorrow, but Lark longed to share her happiness with the sister she loved.

At that very moment, the door to the private room swung open a few inches and Risa stuck her head through the crack. "Got room in there for a very proud aunt?" she asked.

Lark gasped in delighted surprise and opened her arms. Risa flew into them, and Lark had just a glimpse of the man entering behind her—

Her gasp this time was of shock, for Wes Sherborn was the last person on earth she expected to see. Jared seemed equally surprised; in his case, it was almost as if he'd expected someone else. But his greeting was cordial, although these two men had not met since the day Jared carried Lark away.

Risa's eyes were misty with emotion. "I hope you don't mind me bringing Wes," she said, swiping at damp cheeks.

Lark, completely mystified, shook her head. "No, of course not. Although why he'd want to be here is beyond me."

Wes stepped up behind Risa and slid his arms around her waist, his smile sunny. "I have my reasons," he said in a teasing tone.

That's when Lark knew. She gaped at the two of them; Risa was the love of Wes's life—and vice versa! Laughing, crying, hugging, she wished them all the best. Automatically her glance searched for Jared, wanting to share her happiness with him, but he had slipped from the room, apparently wanting to give them privacy.

Lark squeezed Risa's hand. "But why did it take you both so long to acknowledge your feelings?" she scolded.

Risa and Wes looked equally sheepish. "Guilt, mostly," she admitted. "It was important to me that Tony know Wes wasn't 'the other man' in our breakup, because he wasn't. My marriage was a mistake from day one. When I realized how attracted I was to Wes, I resisted for all I was worth. First because of you, Lark—I thought you were just skittish, that you'd come to your senses and see his sterling qualities.''

She smiled ruefully. ''I think the Mallorys and the Sherborns betrothed the two of you at birth, and I couldn't see myself as a spoiler. Father honestly considered you and Wes a match made in heaven. When you married Jared instead, Wes and I waited as long as we could in hopes that Father would eventually get over his bitterness.'' She shook her head sadly. ''I'm no longer sure that he ever will.''

That was Lark's second regret: that she'd never been able to make peace with her father. Now, Risa, his favorite, was estranged from him, too.

It was the only area of Lark's life where she still felt like a failure, although she realized her husband would never forgive Drake Mallory, not even for her.

She'd never ask him to try. Jared Wolf was a proud man and she'd rather die than see him humble that pride for anyone or anything.

Slowly over almost two years of marriage, Lark had pieced together most of the details of her father's relationship with the Wolf clan. Drake hadn't bought Wolf Cabin for a family retreat but as a trysting place for his occasional marital infidelities. Only after her mother discovered its existence did her father try to cover his tracks by taking his wife and children there.

Lark realized now that her parents' marriage had been in trouble years earlier than she'd thought. Even so, she missed her only living parent, especially now that she was a wife and mother and no longer feared falling back into old self-destructive habits.

If wishing could make it so—

The door opened again and there stood Jared—*with Drake Mallory* at his side. Lark and Risa stared, their shock total. Drake's arms overflowed with teddy bears and baseball bats and basketballs and everything else a boy could want; his eyes overflowed with tears, which he tried unsuccessfully to blink away.

He swallowed hard. "I'm sorry," he barked into the stunned silence.

Lark's astonished glance flew to her husband's face. "How—what—I don't understand!"

Jared sighed and rolled his eyes toward the ceiling, then shrugged. "Simple." He gestured Drake Mallory into the room but his gaze never left his wife's. "I love you. This will make you happy. What else can I say?"

Nothing; words no longer mattered. Because of this very special man, Lark Mallory Wolf's life truly *was* perfect.

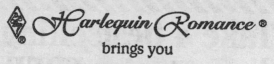

Harlequin Romance ®

brings you

How the West Was Wooed!

We've rounded up twelve of our most popular authors, and the result is a whole year of romance, Western style. Every month we'll be bringing you a spirited, independent woman whose heart is about to be lassoed by a rugged, handsome, one-hundred-percent cowboy! Watch for...

Take 4 bestselling love stories FREE

Plus get a FREE surprise gift!

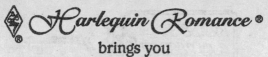

BRIDE'S
BAY RESORT

UNLOCK THE DOOR TO GREAT ROMANCE
AT BRIDE'S BAY RESORT

Join Harlequin's new across-the-lines series, set
in an exclusive hotel on an island off the coast of
South Carolina.

Seven of your favorite authors will bring you exciting stories
about fascinating heroes and heroines discovering love at
Bride's Bay Resort.

Look for these fabulous stories coming to a store near you
beginning in January 1996.

Harlequin American Romance #613 in January
Matchmaking Baby by Cathy Gillen Thacker

Harlequin Presents #1794 in February
Indiscretions by Robyn Donald

Harlequin Intrigue #362 in March
Love and Lies by Dawn Stewardson

Harlequin Romance #3404 in April
Make Believe Engagement by Day Leclaire

Harlequin Temptation #588 in May
Stranger in the Night by Roseanne Williams

Harlequin Superromance #695 in June
Married to a Stranger by Connie Bennett

Harlequin Historicals #324 in July
Dulcie's Gift by Ruth Langan

Visit Bride's Bay Resort each month wherever
Harlequin books are sold.

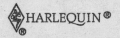

HARLEQUIN ®

BBAYG

Harlequin Romance ®

brings you

Jessica Steele's

#3416 *A Wife in Waiting*

The heartwarming sequel to her November 1995 book, *The Sister Secret*.

Belvia and Josy Fereday are twins. Although they look alike, they're chalk and cheese when it comes to their characters.

Now that Belvia (the heroine of *The Sister Secret*) is happily married, the last thing Josy wants to do is intrude on her newlywed twin. Then Dacre Banchereau offers her an ideal solution—a home, a job and...marriage! But that's one proposal she wouldn't dream of accepting. Widowed and wary, Josy has decided that she just isn't marriage material. But Dacre Banchereau is a patient man. Is it only a matter of time before his wife in waiting becomes a bride in his arms?

Of *The Sister Secret*:

"Ms. Steele pens a touching love story with vivid characterizations, gripping scenes and a powerful conflict."
                                        —*Romantic Times*

JSTEELE

HARLEQUIN®

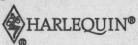